A Weird Fiction Tale:
Age of Wonder

A Weird Fiction Tale: Age of Wonder

Copyright © 2021 by JCC Chavez, Jr.

All rights reserved. This book or any portion thereof may not be reproduced or used in any manner whatsoever without the express written permission of the publisher, except for the use of brief quotations in an article or book review.

This is a work of fiction. Any references to historical events, real people, or real places are used fictitiously. Other names, characters, places, and events are the products of the author's imagination or used in a fictitious manner, and any resemblance to actual persons, living or dead, or actual events and locales is entirely coincidental.

Cover Dragon Artwork by Mestizo Ink Productions

Cover Design and Interior Formatting by Amanda Reid with Melissa Williams Design

ISBN 978-1-7360633-0-9

A Weird Fiction Tale:
Age of Wonder

JCC Chavez, Jr.

Chapter 1

THE SOWING OF TWO SEEDS

Wiggling his little black nose, the young pup scurries across the endless woods. No tree or stone, nor patch of grass is left untouched by his keen sense of smell.

Milo is a tiny white-furred, brown spotted Chihuahua, an eager pooch with an insatiable hunger for knowledge. His paws and snout are covered deep in mud and moss. He has been in the woods by the outskirts of the town, searching for an important ingredient necessary for his amateurish potions experiment.

The eleventh centennial of the Age of Wonder is but a few days away, and the grand magus, Grandmaster Harryhausen, has proclaimed his search for an apprentice. Excited, curious whispers engulf the entire town, for only one fortunate person or beast may be bestowed with the honor of inheriting the "Horned One's" magickal legacy. Milo has made it his mission to be that one fortunate individual.

He has spent a many endless nights studying countless magickal scriptures, reciting ancient incantations, and honing his latent magickal abilities. He is an eager pooch, after all, often letting his youthful zeal carry him astray from simple concepts, like time and commitment.

Dusk approaches fast. From morning's early mellow air to the cool mist of night, he has tirelessly been searching for the one ingredient which will elevate his simple potion from mere amateur concoction to extraordinary genius.

On the eve magick bled from the skies and blessed the lands across the world with wonders, many natural occurrences have since transcended above the norm onto the realm of the supernatural.

Beasts were given sentience, and the land nurtured mystical ores—coined myore by the polymaths of the time—of limitless potential and vegetation life ripened with unimaginable splendors. Mandrake, in this case, produces heightened hallucinogenic effects which can warp the deep bowls of the psyche. It produces the desired effect Milo needs for his potion, for he has concocted a rather crude, yet inventive mix.

The potion consists of many crude ingredients: a single white myore stone, crushed Tortoise Snail shell (a relatively small fraction that won't hurt the gargantuan snail), Lilly pollen, Hallowed Waters from Shrine of the Old Green Ones and mandrake. He has gathered all ingredients at great expense, but mandrake is the key ingredient.

The sunlight dims along with Milo's patience. He is about to resign himself from the fruitless venture. But one last sniff along a marshy willow tree where a batch of Groove Shrooms grows about its under roots, and his little black nose finally catches a whiff of the mandrake.

His little brown ears perk up in earnest. Wagging his little white tail happily, Milo sinks his little white paws into the moist soil. Holding firmly to the mucus lathered body of the mandrake, Milo yanks it out. The wormlike mandrake wiggles and shrills, frantically trying to free itself from the Chihuahua's grasp. Milo lets out a small, jovial bark as he places the mandrake inside a nicely sealed jar, which he then places inside his trusty satchel.

Dirty, exhausted, but overjoyed, Milo dusts his little paws.

His ears are suddenly drummed with the sound of the town church bell. The thundering chime sends his ears and tail jolting up with alarm. He is late for a particularly important meeting with his brothers. Milo gathers his belongings hurriedly, and dashes on all fours down the hill towards the lively town.

The town is overtaken with loud protests from the townsfolk—Men and beasts alike. The turmoil of an impending war looms above the town like a thunderstorm that ushers in a great extinction.

For many suns and moons, there have been loud, collating talks of discontent and rebellion from the Simian United Front, the Stallion Commonwealth and the Republic of the Second Sun. Milo does not understand nor cares much for political scuffles and banter. He is too enamored with his youthful optimism. To him, the idea of impending war is as fantastical as magick itself.

But his curiosity is insatiable. So, he decides to squeeze in between a small crowd that has gathered around a Tinker and Trinket shop window. An old tele-transceiver broadcasts the recent speech from the Simian United Front's current spoke-beast.

The event is being broadcasted from the Republic of the Second Sun's capital hall, with a podium placed at the hall's main entrance steps. At the forefront of the podium is a gibbon. His stern, rough demeanor disguises a sharp, calculating mind. Known for his ambitious nature and borderline fanatical ideological beliefs, the gibbon known as Gideon takes the centerstage of the broadcast.

> *My fellow Simians and other gentle-beast, I am here today not to encourage war, but to enlighten on the need for change and revolution. The council has once again declined our rights to the Southern Highland Woods. They presume to have a right to deny us what is rightfully ours. Their decision is biased in favoring The Stallion Commonwealth, who have, since before the Eve of Wakening, been under the heel of servitude and oppression. A position the Stallions hold with callous glee. The council is marred with bigotry and delusions of equality, marginalized*

by the race of Men who continue to oppress the rights of all beasts. Men . . . their time as the dominant species has long since ended. They call us gibbons lesser apes, a title of oppression we shall take from them and make our own. Lesser implies inferiority, but we shall make it something grandeur, respected, and feared. I speak now to all my Simian brothers and fellow beasts; we shall be oppressed by an inferior species no more! Henceforth, I proudly accept the burden of leadership and promise to lead all my people into a new age of prosperity and glory as Gideon the Lesser!

Fearful murmurs follow after the tele-transceiver goes dark and silent. Gideon's words only help elevate the anxieties of war. Milo recognizes Gideon as a fellow scholar. Although he finds the gibbon highly displeasing now, at one point, he recognized his brilliance and articulation when trying to spur the passions of the masses.

"Quite a fiery tongue that monkey has wouldn't you agree, Milo?" Boreas is a plucky, sable Hog. His kind, bespectacled face smiles down at the petite Hound.

The Hog is a curator at the Bartleby's Bizarre and Other Exotic Eccentricities Museum. For months, Boreas lent his council to Milo, helping the young Hound with his magickal training. His position gave Milo access to ancient scrolls and manuscripts containing complex, exotic incantations. He is a robust, jolly, and humble Hog. An exceptionally good friend to Milo.

"Perhaps, but he lacks that panache of refined vulgarity, like a tubby little pig I know," Milo replies in good humor to the plump Hog. Boreas chuckles, his flabby body jiggling with glee.

"Oh, ho-ho, watch yourself pooch, don't let the missus hear you say that, or it'll be the pigpen for me again." A refined scholar, Boreas, is renowned for his vast knowledge of ancient magickal artifacts and scriptures. Knowledge rivaled only by his rather dirty choice of words, which one too many times have earned him reprimands from his wife, the Doe, Olive Honeydew.

"I think your sloppy tongue will do the job for me, old friend." Milo winks.

Both Hound and Hog join in a small laugh.

Greetings aside, Milo reaches inside his satchel and pulls out a nicely rolled parchment freshly resealed with wax. He hands the parchment over to Boreas, who nods in gratitude.

"Thank you for letting me borrow it, my pungent friend, and I say that respectfully."

The Hog takes no offense to Milo's remark, for his vulgarity is only rivaled by his humorous nature. He simply gives a brushed gesture as he chuckles. "Very funny, my tiny friend. Glad to be of service to a fellow scholar. Say, were you able to find that mandrake?"

"Aye, took me all day, but I got it." Milo pulls the jar out from the satchel and gives his plumpish friend a peek at the worm-like mandrake.

"Oh ho-ho-ho, slippery little fella, isn't he? Congratulations are in order, my flea-ridden mutt." Boreas exclaims gleefully. He then lifts Milo off the ground in an air-tight bearhug.

Milo can't help but chuckle at the gesture. Feeling breathless, he brushes him off.

The overzealous Hog accompanies Milo down the town streets, immersed in conversation. The streets are lit with fiery protest, tensions of war spring high in the air and suffocate the peaceful normalcy of the town. Milo sighs heavily. The sight of societal collapse amid the corruption of fear over honor fills him with melancholy.

"Do you believe in what Gideon says? About the need for revolution without war, I mean." He inquires to the thoughtful Hog. "Is such a thing possible?"

Boreas is taken slightly aback by the young Hound's question. He gives an uncomfortable chuckle and anxiously rubs his neck, foolishly attempting to hide his discomfort. "Since when do you share an interest in political affairs?"

"I don't. But it's hard to ignore the effect the Simian's strong beliefs are having on the public." Milo firmly restates his question. "Well? Do you find truth in what Gideon says?"

Boreas sighs in resignation. He knows too well the futility in ignoring the inquisitive Hound's tenacity.

"It's foolishly naive actually, to envision change without war, much less bloodshed. Even in the absence of thought, war exists. A seed cannot grow and flourish into a tree without rupturing the soil that nurtures it. War is only natural, even a beautiful ugliness at times." Boreas wipes clean his spectacles, a nervous jitter of his. "The eleventh centennial is dawning over the horizon, just as a new seedling slowly forces its way out from the earth. The Age of Wonder approaches its end, and I fear war is inevitable, old friend."

The Hound and Hog reach the town square where crowds of Men and beasts debate furiously amongst themselves. Gideon's recent speech, the Southern Highland Woods controversy, and the recent tribal uprisings are the topics thrown about roaring voices. Milo turns to both Man and beast. Their distinctions melt and meld until the Hound can no longer tell them apart.

"Gideon's a brilliant beast. Shame his bigotry overshadows his more admirable qualities. Anyone with a fraction of reason can see that he's only using the territory debacle to fuel ill sentiments against the race of Men amongst noble beasts. If the Council of Suns would only—" Milo's outburst is cut short by Boreas' patting paw over the Hound's shoulder.

"Now, now, no need to concern yourself with such trivialities. After all, tomorrow is a big day, old boy. Tomorrow you'll be announced as Grandmaster Harryhausen's new apprentice!" The Hog boasts proudly at the top of his lungs.

"That's still up to debate, my boorish,

cholesterol-challenged friend. The preliminaries alone were challenging. Out of twenty, only myself and three others are left. I'm afraid the wee competition is nothing short of ravenous, and with an appetite mightier than this tiny pooch." Milo differs half-heartily.

The Hog looks down at the young Hound sternly.

"None of that old boy. Harryhausen is known for his fierce devotion to his craft. Being one of the finalists alone speaks bounds about your gifts and talents." The Hog kneels next to Milo and holds him firmly by the shoulders. Boreas encourages the youth's ambitions. "You're hungrier than the lot of them talentless lummoxes, and they lack the one thing you have: Conviction for the greater good."

Milo shows his gratitude with a happy tail wag. "I suppose you're right. Tomorrow we'll know for sure then."

"That's the spirit! It's not the size of the bite that counts, but the thunder of the bark. So, I'm assuming your brother Iggy has taken the news of your magickal venture rather well then?" Boreas worriedly notices the awkward silence that follows his question. It is something that does not sit well with his stomach.

Milo only creases a cheeky grin.

Iggy is one of Milo's older brothers, along with Bobbie. He is the youngest of the three. Iggy's fierce devotion and protective nature toward his two younger siblings are reputable. An opinionative Hound, Iggy, can be overly critical about his brothers' life choices. Furthermore, the rabid Hound is incredibly distrustful and self-indulgently ignorant towards anything mystical. Milo is more than aware that Iggy would have never approved of his coveting an apprenticeship with the Horned One.

Unable to look Boreas straight in the eyes, Milo lowers his head shamefully with his ears slightly dropped backward.

"He's . . . okay with it. Especially since I haven't quite told him yet."

The Hog's eyes ignite with palpable concern. He can hardly control the stutter quivering his mouth. "B–b–b–beg pardon?"

"He doesn't know because I haven't told him. But I will tomorrow—promise I will." Milo vows desperately to the overanxious Hog.

Boreas is most unpleased with what he has just heard.

"Boy, you stay away from me and make

no mention of my involvement to that rabid brother of yours. You hear me?!"

"Boreas you're being a tad overripe, wouldn't you say?" Milo can't blame the Hog's outburst. If anything, he sympathizes, certain his reaction would be no different if their roles were reversed.

"Last time I tampered with your brother's delicate temperament, he bit me on the left side of my arse! Took four grown men to pry his jaws off my ham. I couldn't sit for a week after!" The Hog pants hotly. "Why haven't you told him? Oh boy, I have no desire to be near you, nor in town, nor this bloody continent when you tell him!"

"Well, you know how he feels about magi, faeries, and magick. He finds it all a bore, rubbish best left unmentioned, much like anything he doesn't quite understand. Besides, there's nothing he can say or do to change my mind at this point. My mind is made up. It's what I want. And don't worry, I'll be mum on your involvement with Iggy. This I vow on my honor as a proud Hound." Milo reassures, which seems to calm the Hog a tad. "Besides, I'm certain after he's given his two cents, his tedious honorable nature will make him accept my decision."

"Before or after he tears off your tail and strangles you with it?" Boreas asks with a smidge of cold sarcasm.

"Knowing my brother, after." Milo replies flatly.

Pyres of uncertainty fuel the anxieties of the unknown tomorrows, and the crowds of protesters turn livelier and more tumultuous. Milo and Boreas are nothing more than spectators to the unraveling decay of reason as chaos takes form and engulfs their world in thunderous screams of savagery. While the world preoccupies itself with the ideals of revolution, the Hound and Hog focus on the consequences the seeds of the now will reap in the morrow.

The Hog grows more worried with the crowds' erupting unrest and the surly mood of their surroundings. "We best be making our way home, old boy. The atmosphere is getting quite distasteful for my liking."

"You be safe, my gluttonous friend, give my best to the missus." Milo nods in agreement.

"Where are you heading off? Getting too rowdy to be anywhere that isn't home."

"I'm meeting my brothers at the pub," Milo replies. "I'm late as it is."

"I see. Well, be safe, the lot of you."

The Hound and Hog bid one another farewell and disappear into the masses of beasts and Men. As they distance from one another, Milo overhears the Hog shout back at him through the horde of screams.

"And make no mention of me to your hellhound of a brother." The Hog gives him a firm reminder. "Couldn't sit for months. I enjoy a good sit down from time to time, you know. I got twenty stitches because of him. Damn rabid mutt, no sense of propriety . . ."

Boreas' snorting voice slowly fades, devoured along with the rest of the countless screaming, snarling voices. Milo can't help but chuckle, even in the sea of madness brewing around him.

Chapter 2:
A Hound's Honor

The Lion's Den is always open late. The pub offers fine wines and spirits along with finer cuisine. The atmosphere inside its wooden walls is a stark contrast to the town square, oddly friendlier and quieter, and its patrons a tepid blend of beasts and Men.

Stallions congregate in the far corner of the pub. Proud, egotistic creatures, Stallions often prefer the company of their own. Men and other beasts intermingle by the booths and bar, while a pack of Hounds is immersed in a tense poker game under the smoke and dim, green light.

Murmurs of simpler concerns spread across the pub. Milo casually passes between two arguing Men; he is tiny and easily goes unnoticed by the two burly vagrants.

"Oh hoy, over here little brother!"—a

smooth, silky voice calls out to him. Milo turns to a booth near the bar. There, the scruffy Terrier whose creamy fur stands out like a great white dot amidst the somberly lit pub waits for him patiently.

Roberto "Bobbie" Gael Barraza is the middle sibling of the three. Not emotionally incendiary as Iggy, nor passionate as Milo, Bobbie is the mellower of the three. A trait that has conditioned him well into playing mediator during bitter arguments between his two other brothers. Quiet, loving, and insightful, Bobbie is Milo's confidant, the only sibling privy to his magickal extracurricular activities.

Milo joins his brother by the booth. Bobbie grinds tobacco into a wooden oak pipe, wiggling his pink nose as he does so. The scruffy Hound cocks a brow and gives the young pup Milo a scolding glare with a honey, nut-brown eye.

"You're late, fashionably late. You know how our beloved older brother hates tardiness." Bobbie gives him a fair warning.

"Sorry, I got caught up looking for the mandrake, and I was chatting with Boreas on the way over here. Not to mention the protests outside were a drag." Milo explains timidly.

Bobbie quickly raises a paw, and gestures silence.

"Relax, you won't be licking any wounds today. Luckily, those protests are proving beneficial to your well-being, little bother. All this worrisome chatter of war and revolution have Iggy all fired up and distracted." Bobbie takes a few puffs from the lit, smoky pipe, and fumes out a peculiarly fresh scent of autumn mint. "You got your paws on some mandrake I'm presuming it is safe to assume."

Milo nods.

"You're closer to perfecting your potion. Then, I'm safely presuming is safe to assume."

"Indeed, but with everything that's happening lately, it's going have to wait for the moment." Milo laments with a nod.

"Wise and perceptive. Now, I hope you're fully committed to telling our beloved, ill-tempered brother tonight about your—ahem—career path. Given the inconveniences stirring about us, now's the most convenient time to do so. I'm presuming you took the necessary precaution to recite what to say to him already." Bobbie notices Milo's lowered gaze and shaky head.

He grits his fangs against the oak pipe whilst

taking several labored puffs. Bobbie lowers the oak pipe, a calm gesture that causes Milo's tail to curl underneath his bum. The scruffy Hound rubs his eyes, earnest to maintain a cool composure whilst he lectures his little brother.

"Milo, you've got to tell him tonight. The Final Trials of Apprenticeship will commence tomorrow at noontide, and there is a good chance you will emerge as the Horned One's apprentice. You'll tell Iggy tonight unless you wish for tomorrow's joyous moment to be a short-lived one."

"Aye, I hear you." Milo pouts. The petite Hound is still hesitant to tell Iggy about his dabbling in the mystic arts. But he has no choice, lest he breaks his vow to Boreas. "I, um—I'm simply worried we're a tad hasty letting him know tonight. We won't know for sure if I'll be the declared victor until tomorrow. Yes, I think it's best to let him know after the finals and—"

A loud thud silences both Hounds mid-tiff. Their fur stands in static shock. A tray of drinks has suddenly been slammed down on their table. Both Milo and Bobbie exchange worried glances, dumbfounded as to how much of their conversation was heard by their big brother Iggy.

"What are you bitches babbling about now?" Iggy's hoarse, gravelly voice normally preludes a violent outburst. It intimidates all Men and beast alike, even his two younger siblings.

Ignacio "Iggy" Hidalgo Echevarria is a Boston Terrier. An honor-bound, courageous militant Hound with a foul temper to match his fierce familial loyalty and bravery. He takes great pride in his role as eldest of their close-knit pack and as a decorated member of the Hound Brotherhood. All his life, he has protected his brothers, for behind his gruff, stern exterior lays a tenderness for both and a begrudging nobility for fairness.

A Chihuahua, Terrier and Boston Terrier sit in a dimly lit booth. Namesakes may vary, and blood is unbinding as their appearance, but all three are bound like true brothers. A proud pack united through heart and soul.

Orphans, since pups, faith brought them together after a devastating fire engulfed their town, many echoing ticks of the clock ago. The raging inferno turned their blood families to frail ash. But both Milo and Bobbie were saved from the fires by Iggy. Fear of the flame has burned deep within Iggy from that day to this, but it also forged a strong newfound family, welded strongly together by something deeper than the most powerful magicks.

The gruff Hound has brought the drinks to the table. Knowing both his brothers' taste, he took it upon himself to order their drinks.

"Crimson Pike for my fuzzy little man," Iggy passes a red ale beer to Bobbie.

"And a dark frizzy pop for my absent-minded genius of a little brother." He nudges Milo playfully for his tardiness and passes a cold dark soda to him due to his distaste for booze and spirits.

They imbibe their drinks in awkward silence. Bobbie nudges his head Iggy's way, near the point of cracking it, pestering Milo tirelessly to speak up about the events to unfold the following morning. Iggy pays no notice to the two as they argue mutely, much too preoccupied indulging his thirst. The gruff Hound carelessly chugs the mug of dark Buttercream Ale and licks the foam off his muzzle. The dry thirst shriveling his tongue quenched, Iggy finally catches his two brothers tossing glances of caution to one another betwixt an offbeat silence. His flaring nostrils catch a whiff of suspicion.

"What are you two mongrels whispering

about like old ninnies? Come now, no secrets." Iggy darts a look at Bobbie. The scruffy Hound nervously puffs at the oak pipe like a coughing locomotive. He then shoots back to Milo, who instinctively dodges his dominating glare and pays closer attention to the yet untouched mug of fizzy pop.

"Must be something good, big, and unpleasant if neither of you is willing to spill it. You little bitches." Iggy snarls. He then points to Milo. "Mind telling me why you late, runt?"

Milo unpins his fangs from his tongue, intent with finally spilling the details of his recent flirtation with magick and desire to be the chosen apprentice of the grand magus, Grandmaster Harryhausen. But regrettably, such pluckiness is waylaid by a loud, splintering thrash of angry Simian hoots and equine brays.

Down at a dark corner of the pub, near the billiards, a pinto Stallion wrestles with an enraged gibbon. Many unfriendly and uncivilized words are exchanged between both beasts as tables are torn in half, glasses shattered, and fluids spilled over fine oak floors. Primal urges are baited, and adrenaline boils blood hot with hate. Fortunately, the pub's staff is quick to cut the scuffle short, and both beasts and their parties are hastily booted out of the pub.

Tensions cool, though ripples of rage remain.

Iggy slams his tiny fists on the table and gives off a soft growl. "That flea picking, grub gorging, silver tongued monkey has done it! War is inevitable. Bobbie, what say you brother? What does that glitter dame of yours have to say about all this?"

Iggy has been highly involved with the recent political turmoil. He reserves no love or respect for Gideon the Lesser. In Iggy's own dogged opinion, the gibbon revolutionary is nothing but a blatant opportunistic bastard who further festers the contempt delusions of the unheard voices. In his mind war has already broken out, and the Hound Brotherhood is prepared to lend its support to the Republic of the Second Sun.

"*Lady* Tumnus," Bobbie takes a short puff from the pipe before continuing, "is hopeful that diplomacy can sort out this sordid mess without bloodshed. But I, a far more pragmatic creature, disagree with her naïve opinion . . . respectfully, of course. Gideon's appointed himself the Lesser of the Simian United Front, such an unreal title foretokens a very real horror—war."

"Aye," Milo interjects. "Gideon and I once shared a short but respectful friendship in days of yore. He's a fiendishly clever gibbon with a lash and capable tongue when subjecting the ignorant crowds. Though his razor wit is blunted by his anger for the race of Men, Gideon's still the most willful beast I've ever known, even for a Simian."

Iggy growls rabidly and takes another gulp of Buttercream Ale. "Dishonorable prick is what he is. Damn arse scratching monkey stirs nothing but unnecessary madness whenever he flaps that second anus, he calls a mouth. Fierce words can't conceal the foul stench of the shite he spouts." He angrily hawks a ball of phlegm onto the floor, "He speaks of honor when he knows naught about it. He has no honor and a beast without honor . . ."

"Is nothing more than a mindless animal." Both Milo and Bobbie chant unenthusiastically.

Iggy growls irately. "Funny, real funny bitches."—he grumbles, unamused.

Milo knows he can no longer prolong the inevitable, especially with Bobbie giving him the evil eye throughout the entire night. He takes a deep breath and gives a quick prayer to whichever of the seven Old Green Ones may be listening. "Despite this unsightly ugliness happening, tomorrow is going to be a rather special day, big brother. A really special day . . . for me."

Iggy gives the shaky Milo a puzzled look. "Is that so? Now, why is that runt?"

"Well, um . . ." He turns to Bobbie, trying to bully him for aid with droopy ears and pleading puppy eyes.

Bobbie dodges Milo's plea for help and preoccupies himself with the pipe cupped in his paws. He shrouds himself from Iggy with a thin cloud of tobacco smoke. Through the slowly thinning white cloud, the scruffy Hound lifts a brow at Milo.

The petite Hound reads Bobbie's gesture clearly. He alone must confront Iggy just as a grown Hound should. But in all modesty, he too knows that Bobbie wishes to avoid Iggy's reputable angry outburst.

"Wuss."—Milo snarls back at Bobbie. Abandoned, he continues alone. "I'm sure you've heard, Grandmaster Harryhausen's in search of an apprentice. Well . . ."

"Well, what?" Iggy surmises what his little

brother is about to tell him. A foretokening vein pulsates eagerly above the ill-tempered Hound's brow.

Milo gulps a deep, moist breath. He tries his best not to stutter like a frightened pup. "I, um, I've secretly been studying the mystic arts and practicing ancient spells for years now—late at nights, away from home and . . . you. And for the past four months, I've made it through the apprenticeship preliminaries with flying colors. Tomorrow morn the Final Trials of Apprenticeship will take place at Grandmaster Harryhausen's citadel, where I'll be competing against the other three finalists for the honored title. Well, um, that's pretty much it . . . I think."

Iggy gawks wordlessly. Every joint in his dwarf body is petrified, all but his right eye, which twitches madly. Milo's surprising confession is unexpected and unsavory. His blood boils to a steam. The hotness fogs his thoughts and blisters his tongue.

"I—I wanted to tell you sooner, really I did. I also thought about quitting cold, but Bobbie said I've demonstrated a great aptitude for magick and that I'd be a fool to let such a gift lay dormant." Milo adds forlornly.

Bobbie glares at him disapprovingly, befuddled that Milo has fingered him as an unwitting accomplice. Now he too is exposed to their big brother's wrath.

Iggy darts Bobbie with a stern glance. He growls rabidly at the chimney puffing, scruffy Hound.

A breath of silence stretches over a moment, the murmurs and other sounds of the pub go silent. The silence is torture enough, and Iggy only claws at the table, splintering the wood— thin threads curl around his stiff paw.

After what feels like an eternity, he finally ushers a single word. "No."

"No, what?" Milo isn't surprised by Iggy's response, but nonetheless, chooses to stand indignant.

Bobbie glances between the two, jitterily puffing smoke from the pipe without a breath to spare.

"No brother of mine is going to meddle in fairytale shenanigans. I forbid it, Milo!" Iggy has never been one to handle things delicately nor gracefully. He forces his authority down on the rebellious Milo with stern doggedness. He then swings back to Bobbie.

The scruffy Hound's wish to remain invisible is quashed with a hoarse bark.

"And you, you ragged, filthy mop of a dog, you knew about this?!"—Iggy snarls. Strings of drool drip from the edge of his muzzle.

"The hell you say! Why not?" Milo stands defiantly. He leaps atop the seat on his hindlegs. Bobbie continues to puff away at the pipe. "Iggy, this is what I want, and I'm exceptionally good at it. I have a better chance at this than any beasts or Man I know. It's a chance of a lifetime, with the Horned One no less."

"Magick is far too dangerous and unpredictable. It's not some mindless animal you can tame and cage. All magick has ever done is wreak havoc and chaos." Deep down, truth be told, Iggy only wants what is best for his little brother. Though he would not admit it openly, he greatly admires and respects Milo's assertiveness. Regardless, he refuses to sway from his decision.

"But that is because we haven't learned to harness it yet. Eleven centuries have passed, and we've hardly made any significant progress in exposing magick's true splendors." Milo won't back down either. A passionate Hound and scholar at heart, his boundless appetite for knowledge fuels his argument tenfold. "If we learn to harness magick to its full potential, the possibilities to better the lives of all sentient beings will be limitless."

"Understand it?! All we needed to understand from magick was learned firsthand eleven centuries ago. When this fairy dust first hit the world, madness ensued." Iggy drools worriedly. He knows Milo won't back down from this argument. He fears for his little brother's safety, for he is aware of the risks Milo may face during the final trials. "You, who likes to dip his thick skull inside books, should know the history of the Eve of Wakening better than anyone. Bloodshed and anarchy ran amuck. The whole world was turned topsy-turvy, tainted, and malformed."

"And what are we?" Milo inquires stoutly.

"What . . .?" Iggy was never one for debate, due to the occasional override his emotions have on his reasoning.

"Are we not malformations then? Byproducts of unholy depredation upon the natural order?"—Milo asks more firmly.

"Come again, runt." Iggy is flabbergasted by Milo's keen words.

"Magick might've rained chaos upon the

world, but it also blessed beasts with awareness and intelligence, along with profound ignorance it seems." Milo isn't sure what has overcome him. He has never been so brazenly outspoken or disrespectful towards his older brother. Perhaps it is the air of revolution and looming shadow of an impending war. Whatever it is, he won't back down. "We need to decipher the mysteries magick holds. We got to move beyond the shroud of blissful ignorance to comprehend what our world has become. The apprenticeship with the Horned One is an opportunity for me to contribute for a better tomorrow."

Iggy has nothing but great admiration for Milo at this moment. The often shy and compliant pup suddenly demonstrates vast growth and courage. "That was a beautiful speech, words I don't fully comprehend nor care to understand. But I stand by my decision, little brother . . . no. Ignorant I may be, but ignorance can often be the smart thing."

Milo's ears droop in defeat. He knows all too intimately his brother's reputable dogged determination. Nonetheless . . .

"You have no honor." Milo blurts under his breath.

"What did you say, runt?" Milo's quick lashed remark hits a sensitive chord within Iggy. For there are many things which irritate the gruff Hound, but to question his honor is at the top of the hit list.

"You always speak of honor, yet your words are ripe with hypocrisy. How can a beast speak of honor when he refuses to honor the wishes of his family?"

Iggy is caught unawares. Flummoxed, he is unable to mutter a word. "You got grit, runt! Where do you get coming at me with that?" He desperately turns to Bobbie for support. "You listening to this?"—he pouts.

Bobbie takes a nice long pause, along with another puff from the pipe. A thick, white smoke shrouds his face. He then speaks calmly. "He has a point, and you know it. Respecting his wishes is the honorable thing to do here."

Milo smiles meekly.

Iggy growls softly. He knows when he is defeated. Composed, he addresses his little brother, respectfully and calmly. "Fine runt, you got me with my tail between the legs and outvoted too, it seems."

Milo wags his little white tail happily. He has finally won over his brother's softer side.

"Wipe that smile off your mug. I ain't done yet." Iggy sighs in frustration, bested by his little brother at last. He feels the years knead him softly. "And . . . I suppose we can be there for you tomorrow to support the biggest mistake of your life. I shan't have my honor questioned. But promise me one thing alone, little brother."

Milo's ears perk up attentively. He stands proudly before his brother. "Yessir?"

"Give them hell. You say you better than good, then prove it. Not to me. Not to Bobbie. Not to anyone that counts for nothing. Prove it to yourself alone, little brother. Tomorrow, show them what hell a Hound can wreck."

His big brother's encouraging words give Milo an upsurge of confidence and conviction, more than before. Bobbie finally lays down the pipe and raises a mug in salute to this momentous occasion.

"Here, here to our little brother." Bobbie proclaims to the entire pub. "The world doesn't know it yet, but the Horned One—Grandmaster Harryhausen—has already found his new apprentice, and his name is Milo Gabriel Mendoza!"

All three Hounds raise their mugs in joy and pride. Mugs all around clink together, overjoyed for what the future might bring. Iggy pulls his brothers in close for a firm, warm hug.

"At the dawn, our brother will achieve a glory undreamed of by any Hound." Iggy bellows fervidly. "Drinks all around!"

An uproar of laughter and cheers engulf the pub, and the remainder of the night is unlike any other night, one to be remembered for years to come by the three siblings. Joyous, merry, and playful chagrin ensue, pouring unto the late hours of the night.

At home, Milo finds himself restless. The celebrative euphoria still surges about his soul. He looks out to the starry night from his bedroom window. Hope gleams off his eyes. All worldly concerns of an inevitable war are set aside, and he burrows himself in the warmth of his sheets and bed. With a content sigh, the petite Hound finally falls asleep and dreams of the possibilities the tomorrow may bring.

Chapter 3:

THE WHIMSICAL LADY TUMNUS

The following morning is a rhapsodic event. The coffee pot steams hot, and the warm, succulent scents of Bobbie's cooking penetrate every corner of the kitchen. Three plates are prepared with artistic precision.

Bobbie has readied all their favorite meals.

For Iggy, a nice juicy, slightly bloody steak with scrambled eggs topped with a gentle dash of pepper and accompanied with a warm cup of dark-chocolate coffee. Toast is spread with a thin layer of cherry jam, coated with a tiny dash of powdered sugar, and a cup of mint tea is set to the side—Milo's favorite dish. As for himself, Bobbie is partial to poached egg snuggled in a salad of spinach, tomatoes, and olives, covered in a light coat of vinaigrette, with a glass of freshly squeezed orange juice.

"Hurry it up, Milo! Lousy vagrant scoundrel. Can't you conjure up a spell to light a fire under your arse, maybe then you'll hurry it up!" Iggy barks at the top of his lungs.

While Bobbie fiddles with his pipe, grinding tobacco into it, prepping it for later indulgence, Iggy tinkers with their audio-transceiver. The static drones to a soft whine. The incredulous Hound has been toying with it since the waking hours, intending to catch Gideon the Lesser's next public speech.

Static crackles and the signal clears. The gibbon's hoarse voice is heard with discomforting clarity.

> *I've been accused of bigotry and hate-mongering towards the race of Men. My fellow gentle-beast, such unsubstantiated accusations, stem only from fear—fear of the unsung truth. The one absolute truth, that revolution against the established order is not mere ideology, but a natural occurrence that is long overdue. In antiquity, godly, vengeful waters purged the world of archaic theologies, purifying it to a state of rebirth. But like a relentless, thriving*

> *virus, the race of Men refused divine decree and persisted with its malicious existence. Men's survival only wrought famine, hatred, and death back into a world reset by the gods. Before the flood, before the plague of Men emerged from the mud, giants of unimaginable size and power, prided themselves as the pinnacle of evolution, much like the race of Men does today, only to be eradicated by fires set forth from the skies. The truth is out my fellow gentle-beast, and the race of Men knows this. They are relics of an age long past. It is only logical that the natural path their existence must spiral down towards is . . . extinction.*

Static crackles and the signal ends.

Bobbie vigorously munches on his meal, unconcerned with what he has just heard. He gulps the final bite, sips some orange juice, and proceeds to lightning up his pipe. He absent-mindedly puffs on the warm tobacco and takes notice of his brother's uncharacteristic silence. Bobbie nods at Iggy, encouraging him to speak his mind.

Iggy growls defiantly and takes a huge, ravenous bite off his steak. The bloody juices of the red meat drip on the table, reflective of the Hound's bloodlust for the gibbon.

He fantasizes about the gibbon's jugular while he chews on the bloodied piece of meat, rabidly.

"That charm speaking, fairy of a monkey. Idiots, the lot of them. Any who listen to the garbage he sings with the least bit of scrutiny are idiots." Iggy angrily slams an open paw over the table. He may be a military Hound, but the idea of whetting hate to trigger a war does not rest well with him. And it does not take a lettered mutt to foresee the bloodshed that will devour untold innocents. "All that self-righteous, mad beast is suggesting is mass genocide, that's the one truth."

"Well, isn't that the truth," Bobbie nods agreeably. "He knows how to prey on the fears and anger of all those weary voices who've gone unheard for far too long. That there is the absolute truth."

Iggy takes a long sup of coffee, pensive over Bobbie's insightful words. "You saying you agree with the grub muncher?"

"Hear me out before you bite my ear off,

brother." Bobbie takes in a couple of soothing puffs. He feels thoughts flow much smoother with a good smoke. "The government has long been accused of marginalization, favoring only Men to the highest chairs of power. To this day and age, not a single beast has ever been elected to a chair in the Council of Suns. This oversight, intentional or not, gives way to whispers of foul play during elections."

The scruffy Hound is well versed in the current political climate. Being an apprentice to a high council member has made Bobbie privy to the current tumult troubling the Council of Suns. Three small rings of smoke fuming from his pink nostrils help conclude his piece. "Do I agree revolution necessitates war? No. But I do concede change is a must and gravely overdue."

The gruff Hound broods over his brother's wisdom, and reluctantly acknowledges the uneasy truth—revolution is coming at the toll of war!

"Aye, you're right. I'm mud deep in my old ways, make no mistake, but I ain't daft. No Man, beast, or magicks can conquer the inevitable tick of time. Alas, Gideon's rhetoric calls for more than growth—he demands the culling of an entire species! Only villains speak of genocide, and I, along with the other Hellhounds of the Hound Brotherhood, won't stand for it." Iggy lifts an ear. He hears the approaching merry steps of Milo coming down the stairs. "Hush now, no need to bitter our little brother's big day with this nonsense."

Bobbie nods agreeably just as Milo rushes down into the dining room, quite shakily.

Milo has been up since before the dawn, reciting every incantation he knows on constant repeat, refreshing his knowledge of various magickal creatures and mentally strategizing on all possible scenarios that may arise during the Final Trials of Apprenticeship. The jibing voices of failure crept into his dreams late at night. Nonetheless, he remains determined to attain the title of apprentice to Grandmaster Harryhausen at any cost.

"Morning." He munches on toast and gulps a bit of mint tea, which has gone cold. There is little enjoyment in his humble meal. As he jugs down the toast, he recites spells—drizzling crumbs on his blue vest—and draws incantation sigils in the empty air with his paws.

"Slow down there. We've got more than enough time runt." Iggy examines his brother's tense, shaky posture and reads nervousness. "Rough night, I'm assuming."

"Sorry, I'm a tad nervous is all. The reality of what today is . . . shook me in my sheets. There's no turning back now, is there? This is—this is my only chance. The chance of a lifetime. What if I blow it?" Milo seeks for reassurance from his brothers, or better yet, an open paw across the face to snap him out of doubt.

"Well, you ain't much of a mutt. Tad too teeny. You're more of a mouseling, nothing too intimidating." Iggy's usual dry humor—very dry—goes unappreciated. Milo is unsmiling.

"This isn't funny, Iggy. An opportunity like this one only comes once in a lifetime." The petite Hound growls. He is in no mood for humor, especially poor humor.

Milo can't shake the thought of going up against the other prospects, some of whom are equally if not more gifted in the mystic arts than he. The preliminaries alone proved strenuous and draining for a Hound of his diminutive height.

For the first trial, the prospects tinkered with basic astral projection. It was an easy feat to accomplish. Well, it was easy for Milo, at least. Unfortunately, ten prospects never floated back to their empty meat, which has since been left comatose and mindlessly drooling.

The second trial almost cost him his life. He was required to conjure up the Fenrir Wolf and bend it to his will. It wasn't an easy spell to master, nor was the construct. Milo came dangerously close to being swallowed whole by the fire beast. Something he did not share with Bobbie, knowing he would've only been pushed to tell their overprotective brother, Iggy. Casting the spell alone left him bedridden for two weeks straight.

Milo spent another two weeks bedridden after the third trial. He and the remaining prospects were required to summon the ambient magickal energies from a spherical controlled field and bend it to their will. The experience was taxing, both physically and spiritually. Iggy had been under the impression he was weathering a tenacious bug . . . for near an entire month.

Out of twenty hopefuls, only four remain.

Only the most talented and gifted prospects remain, each just as ambitious and driven as Milo. The young Hound, though highly gifted, is but an amateur playing with big dogs. Doubt is truly a cruel mistress.

Luckily, the Old Green Ones have blessed him with a brother like Iggy, who always knows how to inspire conviction in the thicket of doubt. Today is no different.

Iggy pulls Milo close and looks him dead in the eyes. "And you'll grasp that opportunity with your paws and own it, little brother. This glory is already yours; you just don't know it yet. So, flick that parasitic bitch of doubt off unto the nothingness like a bothersome tick."

Milo's eyes enkindle with confidence, and the young pooch can't stop his tail from wagging joyfully.

Iggy grunts proudly and tussles Milo's head playfully. "Now scarf down the rest of your meal, you've got a big day ahead and a hearty meal fuels the spirit, the very oil which kindles magick."

The young Hound nibbles what's left of his hearty meal, sips down the mint tea, and rushes out with his essentials. The first one out the door, he leaps in the air with youthful eagerness. Milo calls out to his brothers to follow in tow as he runs ahead in all fours.

Bobbie relights his pipe and takes in a few good puffs of mint tobacco. Iggy barks to the distant Milo—"Compose yourself, runt, and act like a proper beast." Into the town, the three brothers travel, joining the fray of hundreds of citizens clamoring in the morning hustle, going about their daily routines.

The trio makes a quick stop by the town market at Bobbie's behest. The scruffy Hound has been monkeying with a medicinal cocktail of his concoction for weeks, and an exceedingly rare herb rumored to contain unwonted healing properties has just arrived. Men, beasts, they all convene at the market's miscellany of shops and tents. The atmosphere is loud and lively with clientele yelling out their grocery orders. Market owners scream out directions to their helpers and other uninvolved voices yap about everyday squabbles. The distress of protests from the previous night is but a forgotten memory, for the time being at least.

Deep inside the market is a very peculiar booth, Zeke's Magnificent Miracle Remedies and Other Eccentric Oddities, whose owner, Zeke, is quite a peculiar individual himself.

A man with bronze skin, Zeke often sails across the eastern oceans to harvest rare herbs from the unknown regions of the world. He is seldomly seen wearing a shirt; his exposed upper body is covered in scars, evince of vicious attacks from monstrous claws. Zeke is a fearless, tough man—one had to be when trekking through the hostile territories of the Raptor Isles. The lands of the cold-bloods are mysterious as its inhabitants. Few individuals, Men or beasts ever dare travel there with the mere certitude of a ravening death.

Zeke is one of the few rare men to brave the unknown, vicious, and humid waters of the Raptors. His courage—or folly—have benefited him greatly. Whenever he docks back to the great continent alive, his idiocy turns up a good profit.

Bobbie and the bronze man greet one another and briefly chatter about simple things. Formalities set aside, Zeke hands him the rare Bella Furiosa flower. It is an eerily beautiful flower with a golden splendor and ripe with benevolent secrets. Bobbie, a devout herbalist, and medical prodigy hopes to uncover its exotic secrets and brew wondrous remedies for the boon of every furry and hairless creature.

"Hurry it up, will ye!"—Iggy barks impatiently at Bobbie.

Bobbie bids his acquaintance farewell and hands him two pouches of gold as payment for the rare flower. From the market, the brothers head towards Huckleberry's Steam Engine Station. Hastily, the Hounds purchase tickets and wait at the platform to board the hissing steam engine. In a short minute, the pack of Hounds will be whisked away through the forest, past the outskirts of town, deep into the mountains, onward to the hallowed citadel sanctuary of the Horned One, Grandmaster Harryhausen.

Milo gazes out to the horizon. The rising caterpillar smoke of the steam engine nears the platform, but the petite Hound's mind is too preoccupied to care. Endless dangers await him at the Final Trials of Apprenticeship, and Milo, for the first time, grapples with the notion that he might not make it out alive. Should he stutter during a crucial spell or fall prey to the sultry promises of faeries, it would be the last his brothers will see of him. He looks to his two older brothers; he dares not burden them with worry.

A high-pitch whistle signals the huffing steam engine. Rail wheels shrill and steam hisses to a whisper. The engine comes to a halt.

They check in their tickets with the conductor and board the steam engine. The whistle goes off, rail wheels shrill, steam hisses anew, and the three are on their way. Milo peers out from his seat to watch the station platform recede onto the horizon, pondering ever worriedly on who or what he will become upon the return journey.

The steam engine pierces steadfast through the woods. Lush giant sequoias, giants of antiquity and purity, reach high above the heavens as far as the eye can see. Luminous butterflies, relics of bygone dreams, serenade the woodlands with fluttering songs. Such serene beauty lulls the most aggravated of souls. Unfortunately, the motley crew of Hounds is too preoccupied with their worldly concerns to pay it proper admiration.

Bobbie and Iggy engage in a heated conversation, discussing the current turmoil in the air, Gideon the Lesser, the looming shadow of war and anarchy. Milo pays them no attention. Quill clutched tight on paw; he carefully pens the final lines of a complex magickal sequence on a piece of auburn parchment. The scrawled enchantment is a prerequisite key, and the sole means any of the four prospects can gain access through the Horned One's gated citadel.

It is the first unofficial trial in the Final Trials of Apprenticeship, and all sequences must be in the correct order. Not a single sigil must be left out, and the smallest mistake can prove fatal. The petite Hound is meticulous in his craft. Once satisfied with the sigil sequence's accuracy, he rolls it up and places it back inside his satchel. Grandmaster Harryhausen's citadel is still ten stops away, enough time for Milo to peruse through the reams of notes stuffed inside the satchel. He refreshes himself on potions, mystical sigils, and fantastical beasts, specifically the tragic tale of the faery Ariel, one he has recited countlessly with intimate detail.

Every magickal incantation is mouthed mutely in synchrony with every paw movement mimed in the empty air. Milo has become a master amateur, bending the natural laws and magickal energies within his spirit at a whim. He has only to master the petrifying spell of fear. Doubt is a vile, cruel mistress.

Nerves wring high; nonetheless, the rail wheels shrill, steam thins warmly into a mist, and the whistle wails a high pitch. They have finally arrived at their destination.

Two stone statues of the Old Green Ones hold a crescent moon, the Horned One's mystical symbol, by the gate's archway. The gate creaks open on its own as the three Hounds creep towards it. The lifelike detail on the statues beguiles them.

A duo of Clay Golems greets the small pack of Hounds once their paws sink onto the citadel grounds.

Mystical constructs forged by the Horned One, the hulking Clay Golems, deny the Hounds further access. One totters up closer to them and outstretches a massive open hand to Milo. The petite Hound pulls out the parchment from his satchel and cautiously places it atop the Clay Golem's bulky palm. The creature of mud and adobe swallows the parchment and enters a trance under a dim yellow eye glow.

"What's this all about?" Bobbie asks curiously.

"The parchment is part of the Final Trials. If scribed correctly, the incantation will command the golem to let us pass through the gate unchallenged. Took me over a week to perfect it." Milo explains with cautious optimism.

"Looks like your competition is down

by one runt." Iggy points ahead past the two golems to a clay figure of a horrified Stallion.

His name was Augustus, a Stallion proficient in summoning spells and astral navigation. Yet, quite shamefully, incantation structure was not his forte. The poor chap failed to include two sigils, left a phrase or two out, and the order was out of sequence. Milo was fond of the royal colt. He found him to be friendly and a credit to his uppity people.

The Stallion's horrified visage does not sit well with Iggy. His prejudices towards magick are justly reinforced. "You sure the doodles on that paper are flawless? I've got no plans on being turned into a handsome garden statue anytime soon."

"Don't be paranoid." Milo scoffs. "Magick's not cruel, only those who invoke it."

The Clay Golem's eyes give off a soft emerald glow. Milo's enchantment is a success. The constructs move aside and grant the trio access to the citadel's front steps.

Milo is the last to arrive, and the remaining two prospects already wait by the steps. Moreover, the petite Hound is the only one with a party in tow.

Sir Nicolas Fitzroy is an elderly man with

a long silver mane which he always keeps knotted in a ponytail. When he twigs Milo and his brothers, he tugs his shaggy beard absent-mindedly, as is his wont.

There is a rumor spread about Sir Nicolas. He is believed to be a centuries-old immortal of unknown age. The stories whispered say his immortality was acquired through the untethering of his soul. Such sacrifice has left him in a state of deep remorse for countless eons. His knowledge of the mystic arts precedes the Eve of Wakening, with centuries of refined spells at his disposal.

Of all the prospects, he alone went through the preliminaries without shedding a single tear. Milo holds the elderly man in high regard, albeit intimidated by his boundless years of refined magickal ability.

Then there is Religieux Marlfox. An ambitious silver fox drabbed in a dark cloak and a ceremonial ivory mask conceals his face. The mask is engraved at the frons with the ancient chaos sigil, a hollowed eye pierced outwardly with eight arrows. He belongs to the Black Sun Order, a sect whose members are known to practice chaos magick. The order is enigmatic, its size and members shrouded in shadows, leading many to question its very existence as mere fantasy. But the fox's presence is credence to the contrary.

Milo and Religieux Marlfox share a strong hatred for one another. It stems from an incident when Milo openly criticized the fox's flirtation with chaos magick. The fox took offense to the Hound's remarks leading to a physical confrontation. The incident almost expelled them both from the Final Trials of Apprenticeship.

Cold, piercing glances are exchanged between the Hound and the fox.

"I say you must be Milo." A gentle, yet firm, voice calls out from the steps.

All three Hounds look upward towards the steps and notice a powerful woman, staring down at the lot. The woman wears a silky white outfit; it complements her long, flowing dark hair. She tilts her spectacles, squints her eyes to try and get a clearer look at the three Hounds.

"That I am milady. I'm here today for the same reason—" unfortunately, Milo's unable to finish his sentence, for the woman's no-nonsense attitude and impatience rival Iggy's.

"I know why you're here. I wouldn't be a very good assistant if I were caught unawares of your presence or intentions. I'm just puzzled as to whom the other two mutts are." Her name is Artemisia, a loyal aide to the magus, Grandmaster Harryhausen.

Highly devout to her job and proud in her services to the grand magus, the aide is quite the fury with a strong dislike to any deviations from protocol and tradition. Artemisia is much like Iggy. The pair would make a lovely pair if not for being of different breeds.

She examines Milo sternly, most displeased with the presence of Iggy and Bobbie.

"Well, they're my brothers and—" Milo attempts to explain to no avail. He is brusquely cut off again.

"Uh-huh, and they're here because?" Artemisia waves her hand, hurriedly encouraging Milo to explain himself.

"They're here to lend me their support—" the petite Hound is rudely cut short again for the third time in a row.

"You were informed to come here unaccompanied, were you not?" The aide asks snipingly. "This is a delicate matter, you do realize. This is a sacred, ancient tradition wherein a deep honor will be bestowed upon the worthiest of individuals. It's not meant to be a public spectacle."

Milo's patience is infinite, but Artemisia's unflagging badgering is beginning to wear it thin. He is unaccustomed to rudeness. And as far as Milo is concerned, rudeness is unacceptable and intolerable, even when a person—regardless of breed—teeters on the slope of death.

"Uh, I merely wanted to share this momentous and, should fate smile in my favor, a gracious day with my brothers. With all the excitement, I suppose it'd slipped my mind to come alone." Milo keeps his emotions in check. With Artemisia, such a feat is always a constant challenge.

"Curious . . . very well then. Let us hope Grandmaster Harryhausen overlooks this lapse in judgment. Now, you, mutt, as soon as the master exits the citadel, get in line with the other two."

Iggy gnashes his fangs furiously. He mutters many impolite things under his breath. Things that should never be said to a lady, no matter how rude she may be. "Mutt?! I'll show her a mutt in two seconds."

"Easy there, old tyke, this is our little brother's big day. We must be dispassionate towards her, for his sake." Bobbie coolly warns the hot-tempered Iggy.

"Don't take it personally, Iggy. Artemisia can be quite . . . difficult, yet passionate. She's only doing her job." Milo sympathizes with Iggy. Deep down, he wishes to just let his brother loose on Artemisia. But he isn't ready to throw away this golden opportunity.

A booming creek alerts those present to Grandmaster Harryhausen's forthcoming presence. The citadel's two massive, red wooden doors gracefully swing open, and two imposing figures emerge from the cavernous darkness. The grand magus is not alone.

She is elegantly beautiful. Her silky voice enamors all those fortunate enough to be graced by her presence. Garbed in warm autumn colors, the mysterious Witch of Tumnus exits the citadel, immersed in soft, indecipherable whispers with the Horned One. Grandmaster Harryhausen, in contrast, is an imposing figure. Two curled horns sprout from his head, and he wears a black sorcerer's cloak. His emblem, the Crescent Moon, is stitched in fine white lines at the front of his robe.

The Horned One examines the prospects carefully, stroking his long, curly white beard.

His ashen skin accentuates his piercing blackened, nebula eyes. The grand magus fixates an intimidating glare on Milo and his brothers. He lifts a thin, bony finger and signals the aide to his side. The two exchange a few words. The Horned One's glare never strays from Milo. No doubt, he too questions the presence of both Iggy and Bobbie.

With a dismissive wave of the hand, Grandmaster Harryhausen halts their dialogue. He lifts a puzzled, bushy brow and exclaims loudly, "Curious."

"Yo-ho-ho!" the Witch of Tumnus waves at the trio. She strides down the steps and whimsically calls out exclusively to the scruffy Hound, Bobbie. "Yo-ho-ho, is that handsomely rugged pooch my beloved Bobbie?"

"Milady." Bobbie bows to the Witch. He takes her oily hand and kisses it gently.

Aside from being a well-respected council member, the Witch of Tumnus is the leading authority in Herbal and Potions Research, as well as the chief authority of Historical Records of Mysticism and Obscure Curiosities.

For months, the scruffy Hound has been under her tutelage. Through the Witch's wisdom, Bobbie has made several revolutionary medicinal discoveries. In turn, the creamy Hound won notoriety within the Herbalist and Potions Guild. Iggy has not been opposed to Bobbie's apprenticeship with the Witch, considering it did not deal greatly with magick.

"My, my, what a gentle-beast. So, what brings my fuzzy little pup out here today?" The Witch playfully scratches behind the sweetly bashful Hound's ears, much to Iggy's irk who finds such affections beneath a respectable Hound.

"Lady Tumnus, I am honored to be here today, not only to bask in your company but to pledge support for my little brother on this momentous occasion." The scruffy Hound has always reserved an innocent crush for the Witch of Tumnus. It is unsurprising, for the Witch's vivacious beauty has gained her many suitors.

Bobbie steps aside to introduce Milo, rather shyly. "This here is my little brother Milo, one of the remaining four—um, sorry, three prospects. I forgot about the poor chap back at the gate."

"So, this is the little prodigy I've heard about endlessly. A pleasure to make your acquaintance little Milo. Kudos on the Fenrir Wolf summoning spell, by the way." The Witch gives Milo a flirtatious wink, having heard much about him from Bobbie.

Milo bows to the Witch in return. "The pleasure is mine milady, and thank you for your praise, though I'm not sure I deserve it."

"Gifted and modest. My, my, I think I might grow to like you little one. Don't sell yourself short, though. Such a complex spell isn't easy to master. You've tamed a great power that day Milo, at great risk no less. Curious, for one so small to possess a magickal wellspring of a spirit. Not too shabby little doggie." The Witch then creases a mischievous grin at the disgruntled Iggy. "I suppose this makes you the little sunspot Iggy. Aren't you an adorable little grouch, all mad and tough with your little paws crossed?"

The Witch playfully tussles the cranky Hound on the forehead. Not wanting to jeopardize Milo's chances, Iggy just grinds his fangs and smiles forcibly. "Charmed."—he growls.

The Witch flirtatiously giggles, amused with the pouty Iggy. She returns her attention to Milo. "How do you feel, little one? Ready to venture into the bizarre and weird realm of magick?"

"A tad nervous, but otherwise excited

milady." Milo embarrassingly avoids her mesmerizingly beautiful violet eyes. He now understands Bobbie's deep crush for the Witch. She is quite an elegant and charming woman.

"Worry not little pooch. Don't let ole Horn Head fool you with that cold glare of his. He's just playing the old, cranky warlock role." The Witch pivots the Hound's gaze back unto her. Her cool violet eyes meet his. "Besides, defeat only comes to the victors when they let fear into their hearts."

Milo tilts his head in confusion, unsure of what the Witch is referring to. "Beg pardon milady?"

"I sense greatness within you little one, but there's also much fear in your heart. You're afraid of greatness, of how it might change you." The Witch's voice turns serious and resolute. "Don't be afraid, little Milo, for you've already achieved greatness. You just don't know it yet."

"Yes, milady, of course." Milo is unsure how to react toward the Witch's blunt faith. Every syllable runs deep, and glints hope within him.

"Good. I shall expect to hear your name from ole Horn Head's mouth by day's end then." The Witch of Tumnus smiles at Milo expectantly, confident the Hound will surface as the victor by nightfall.

"Beg pardon Lady Tumnus, but Grandmaster Harryhausen wishes to commence with the trials." Artemisia is more tactful and respectful with the Witch, a stark contrast to her treatment of the Hounds from earlier.

The Witch of Tumnus playfully winks at Milo. "But of course, how rude of me. Best of luck, little Milo, although, I doubt you'll need something as frivolous."

A cool, blue mystical aura engulfs the whimsical woman. She blows kisses at the Hounds, including Iggy, and just like that, the Witch of Tumnus vanishes with the winds.

Grandmaster Harryhausen waste no time to address the three surviving prospects.

"Welcome, to my humble abode." Grandmaster Harryhausen's deep and powerful voice ensnares the immediate attention of every beast and Man present. "By the time the sun sets, only one of you shall be honored with the inheritance of my magickal legacy. Be forewarned, such an ambitious pursuit is set in a fine line of life and death, and the path laid before you shall be what you wish it to be. These are the sole words of wisdom I bestow unto thee. Now let us enter my home, from whence only one will emerge as the victor. Gentle-beasts and gentleman, the Final Trials of Apprenticeship have officially begun."

"Now," Iggy grabs both his brothers in a small huddle. The gruff Hound has never been the most pious of beasts. But at that very moment, he prays to absent gods, hoping with a fervor that this won't be the last time they will be together. "Remember little brother, a beast without honor is nothing more than a mindless animal. Whatever the challenge, face it with honor, always true to yourself, and show them what hell a Hound can wreck."

"And don't you forget, we are with you throughout this journey. All the way, always." Bobbie gulps down his sobs. He must be of stone heart for his little brother. "Survival alone won't make you strong. Never compromise who and what you are, therein lies the true strength. You remember this, okay? And . . . come back to us, little brother."

The three brothers embrace one another firmly.

Milo makes empty promises to appease their worried minds, for he is unsure of what challenges lay ahead within the Horned One's domain. He rushes to join the other two prospects as they follow Artemisia up the marble stairs towards the citadel. Milo glances back to his brothers one last time.

Iggy and Bobbie nod encouragingly. Both mask their fears with false smiles.

The large, red wooden doors shut slowly before them. Iggy and Bobbie helplessly watch their little brother enter the magickal realm of Grandmaster Harryhausen. Uncertainty glares back at them one last time from Milo's worried eyes.

Chapter 4:
COVENANT OF THE MAD

The citadel is an intimidating stone structure. The apotheosis of a great magickal dynasty.

Beautiful oil paintings of bizarre and otherworldly beings surround the endless candlelit corridors. Mysterious artifacts of transcendental natures are on display at marble pillars and large stone statues of immaculate detail grace the epicenter of every hallway and crossroads. Stained glass windows bounce with polychromatic patterns on the carpeted stone floors as light bleeds through from the outside. Massive Clay Golems patrol the halls of the citadel, adding an ambiance of eerie, stark beauty.

Milo realizes he has entered unknown territory. A realm wherein the unexpected is to be expected and perceptions of reality are mere shadows of supernatural dangers.

"Now you may peek and admire. You may embrace the awe, which is Grandmaster Harryhausen's treasury, but you will most certainly not touch." Artemisia, the passionate aide, repeats the same statement sternly throughout every level of the citadel they climb. As for Grandmaster Harryhausen himself, he remains silently at the forefront of the group.

Milo catches him every so often, snatching a quick glance back at him with his piercing blackened, nebula eyes. The petite Hound is unsettled. A spidery, chill crawls down the nape of his neck to his spine and unto the very tip of his white tail. He wonders what the Horned One must think of him, a petite Hound trying to bite off more than he could chew.

Grandmaster Harryhausen, much like the Witch of Tumnus, is an enigma shrouded behind a pall of mystery.

He, along with Lady Tumnus, is one of the original Council of Suns and founder of the Republic of the Second Sun. A powerful mystic who emerged from an unknown realm beyond the veil of reality. The Horned One, as he has come to be known, established order in a world wrought in chaos and anarchy. He took it upon himself to establish a sense of cultural identity and pride within the various beasts baptized with consciousness, laying the foundation for the nations that would become the Stallion Commonwealth and Simian United Front.

As consequence he has come to be revered as a god amongst intelligent beasts across the great continent, much to his humble displeasure. For the Horned One never flirted with such childish notions of godhood.

After climbing over a hundred flight of stairs, the group halts by a pair of ebony doors with golden handles. Two more giants hold up a crescent moon above the door. These two statues are twins to the other two Milo saw at the citadel's front gates, but not entirely mirror-images. These pastiches of the Old Green Ones have etched visages uniquely their own, and their gargantuan majesty lays engraved over the stone walls themselves.

Artemisia turns to the prospects with a needled tongue. "All right, all of you, line up next to each other in an orderly manner. Grandmaster Harryhausen will address you momentarily."

The prospects do as Artemisia commands, aligning themselves one next to the other. Sir Nicolas stands in-between Milo and Religieux

Marlfox, much to his relief. Eager and ready, the three prospects stand proudly astute before the Horned One as Artemisia continues with her pompous sermon.

"The three of you are here today because you've demonstrated great proficiency in the mystical arts. I'll advise you that if you found the preliminaries too strenuous, then I sincerely doubt your chances at surviving the trials ahead." She raises a preemptive hand to stall any premature questions from the prospects. "Here forth, Grandmaster Harryhausen will now discuss the details of the trials with you all. You will do good to bite down your tongues until he's finished."

Under a soft poof of golden smoke, three wooden chests manifest before the trio of prospects. Grandmaster Harryhausen is quick to answer the prospect's quizzical looks.

"The chests before you contain contents revealing the nature of each final trial. A fair warning, the first of many, to any of weak conviction. The fortitude of your psyche will be tested beyond its limits. Madness alone will be but a blessing as your will is turned asunder. A severed limb will be a welcomed mercy and hope, but a dim light devoured by living darkness. Now, proceed and open your chest."

The prospects open their respective chest. Within it, they find a key, a flask with parchment and a small marble surrogate of a greater monster. The Horned One surveys the prospects individually, examining each of their marble surrogates whilst he explains the nature of the Final Trials of Apprenticeship.

"At the end of your respective journeys, you're expected to poach a particular component from the creature carved out from the marble surrogate you hold." Grandmaster Harryhausen brushes his frizzy grey mustache and chuckles sinisterly. Cold fear needles the prospects' spines, for when a magus finds amusement, doom can be expected to follow. "Rest assured, the creatures are of greater size and power, and the quest far more perilous than I bother to illuminate."

First, he surveys the elderly man. Sir Nicolas holds up his marble surrogate to Grandmaster Harryhausen—a fierce, enormous Smilodon-like beast with snarling, elongated canine teeth.

"Sir Nicolas seems you are most honored. At the end of your journey, should the fates deem it so that is, you will engage in an elegant, albeit deathly dance with a man-eating were-jaguar. You are to bring me one of its fangs. A word of caution, though. Be ever so graceful with your steps, for a single misstep will reap dire misfortunes upon you."

"I'll keep that in mind, milord." Sir Nicolas bows respectfully to the Horned One.

Secondly, the sly Religieux Marlfox presents his marble surrogate. A massive bipedal avian beast, with an equally massive wingspan and wooden club clasps tightly around its sinewy, clawed hand, lunges into the oceans as it devours a sea serpent. "My, my, seems you shall be riding through the thunderous wrath of the nagual, Lord Cuitláhuac. Do you feel confident, Religieux Marlfox?"

"Aye, Horned One, for my appetite is larger than the fowl's wingspan and my growl more ferocious than its thunderous shriek." The sly, cocky fox proclaims proudly.

"Careful, my slithery friend, for hubris, is a trait reserved only for the foolish." Grandmaster Harryhausen warns with a sliver of disdain for the fox. Sir Nicolas and Milo often questioned the grand magus' tolerance for the fox's mere presence, as his association with the Black

Sun Order is unanimously scorned. "You're to bring me one of the nagual's feathers and Religieux Marlfox, any use of chaos magick shan't be tolerated, understood?"

"Aye, understood." The fox concedes with gnashing fangs.

Finally, it is Milo's turn. The Hound's eyes flare with shock at the sight of his marble surrogate. Every strand of his fine fur stands in needling salute. It is a serpentine beast with bone barbs protruding along the backside of its elongated body, and scales like thorns all round, and from its fanged, gaping maw, the beast spouts out a stream of fire.

The petite Hound is expected to confront a dragon—the mightiest and most feared of creatures.

"Curious," the Horned One towers over Milo. An inquisitive brow crinkles his hoary face when he stares down at the stunned Hound. "The lord of the Ember Swamp Lands, the Marsh Dragon. You will be but a bothersome flea to it. A small annoyance, unfit as an appetizer for its feral appetite. Curious, for such a small Hound to challenge such a mighty beast. Shall the mouse be triumphant? I wonder . . . curious indeed."

Milo is unsure what Grandmaster Harryhausen expects to incite with his cool, condescending attitude and taunts. Nonetheless, the dogged Hound is determined to rise above any challenge.

"Um, milord, what do you wish for me to obtain from the dragon?" Milo asks timidly. The sage mystic merely brushed him aside without ever stating what he is to appropriate from the dragon. Milo begins to ponder if Grandmaster Harryhausen has little to no faith in him, a meager little Hound.

"Hm? Surprise me, little doggie." The Horned One replies nonchalantly. "Curious, indeed."—he whispers again and saunters away.

Grandmaster Harryhausen then motions all prospects to the double ebony doors. "Now, if you will, please pick up your keys. As you might have figured by now, the keys are of an enchanted nature. Mystical keys that will unlock the doors of destiny, initiating your Final Trials!"

Ceremoniously the Horned One bursts the doors open to reveal an emerald room.

Decorative antiquities surround the room, much like every other room and hall before it. At the center, three doors are lined next to one another, each with a hand-carved wooden frame that chronicles various historical milestones of unknown space and time. Artemisia stands by one of the doors and, at her master's discretion, turns the knob to show that the door leads to nowhere, except to the other side of the room.

"As my faithful aide demonstrates, the doors are nothing necessarily special. Alone, each door is just a hollow decorative piece. But, as you have guessed by now, the keys work in conjunction with the doors..." Grandmaster Harryhausen is renowned for his flamboyant, dramatic showmanship. He excitedly pauses for shock value. "... for one component cannot function without the other!"—he booms with open, spread arms.

"With utmost respect Grandmaster Harryhausen, not that we don't appreciate a good show, but may we please dispense with the theatrics and move on." Sir Nicolas cautiously expresses his impatient enthusiasm.

Grandmaster Harryhausen lifts a bony finger of caution. His blackened, nebula eyes fixate on the immortal, older man. "A word of caution then, before we proceed. You three have demonstrated a natural talent for magick, but be advised, no amount of training, nor talent can prepare you for what awaits you. Once the key and knob are turned, behind these doors, you shall find . . . the Microversity."

The prospects turn to one another, flummoxed at what they have just heard.

The Microversity is the black interdimensional stream betwixt the Four Primordial Realms and all known worlds. Its raw magickal energies are said to warp the mental perceptions of the untrained. To enter such a magickally raw, oceanic plateau is widely considered suicidal. Even some of the most powerful, seasoned warlocks and witches have been known to have lost their minds traveling through its magickally oversaturated depths.

For once, all prospects have found common ground—absolute fear.

"Are you mad, Horned One?" Religieux Marlfox protests snarly to the mad notion. "Everyone knows, not even the mad would dare dwell into the Microversity."

"I say, milord, as much as it sickens me to do so, I find the fox's protest agreeable." Sir Nicolas responds in equal defiance.

"Is that so?" The jocular Horned One maintains a cool demeanor. Strangely, he finds amusement in the two prospects' cowardice. He then turns to Milo, who, up to that point, has chosen to remain quiet on the subject. "What say you little doggie? Am I mad?"

Instinct warns Milo to consider his next words carefully. Should Grandmaster Harryhausen find his soundness disagreeable, he might end up a clay figure like poor Augustus. But the Hound is never one for intimidation, shyness perhaps. And Milo has never feared to speak his mind justly.

"Aye, you are mad. The Microversity is dangerous, even to a veteran mystic such as yourself. To expect amateurs like ourselves to risk our lives so callously in hopes of attaining vast knowledge is but the logic of a madman." Milo, for the first time, looks directly into Grandmaster Harryhausen's blackened, nebula eyes. The piercing glare burrows deep into his soul, and he is unafraid. "But we are just as mad—mad for assuming you'd bestow your legacy unto anyone but the mad."

The Horned One nods agreeably, impressed with Milo's bold statement. "Well, there you have it. Only the mad may proceed henceforth. I ask you then, have the mad alone congregated here today?"

"Aye." The prospects respond in unison.

None wavers to the dangers which lay ahead, and none is willing to be bested by the competition.

Milo takes a sigh of relief. He was certain Grandmaster Harryhausen would blast him into oblivion. But sincerity pardoned his boldness and staved the Horned One's wrath. The petite Hound titters, he is truly mad to continue onward, they all were. Then again, only the mad can breach the finiteness of memory and transcend onto the annals of history.

"Now," Grandmaster Harryhausen announces bombastically. "Prospects, to your doors."

They each approach their respective door with a key on hand and paws.

"Once you have successfully exited the Microversity—if the fates deem it so, that is—open your sealed parchments. It will contain detailed instructions on the next phase of the Final Trials." The Horned One then commands them to insert their keys into the keyholes with but a wave of his bony hand. "Now, turn your keys. May the Death Gods grant you mercy with a blind kiss upon your souls for their harvest is ever so timeless and restless."

Milo turns his key and opens the door. He peers through it and sees not the other side of the room. Pitch darkness greets him, and a cold breeze gingerly brushes his face. His little black nose tickles at the whiff of the Microversity's raw, primal magickal energies. He takes in a deep breath and musters what futile courage his tiny body wombs. On all fours, simultaneously in unison with the other two prospects, Milo lunges into the dark void, into the uncertain shadowy chaos of the Microversity.

Chapter 5:

SHADOWS OF THINGS TO COME

The world disappears behind Milo in a great silence. He floats into a descent wherein he dives onto an ocean of intense darkness where all is one in a great, eternal now.

The Microversity is the dark magickal torrent which segregates and tethers the Four Primordial Realms and known worlds outside Milo's. It is mysterious, as it is dangerous. Its infinite raw magicks snare, twist, and tear to tatters soul and spirit, making it impossible to fully perceive the mimicry of space except as a chaotic mirror of those very souls who imprint upon it.

It is everything and nothing. Time is infinite and finite. Past, present, and future all converge and collide like a tapestry of chaos and order.

The trench of infinity, the Microversity, has

scarcely been explored for it is incapable of singularity. Only the strong of mind and mad dare to swim through the amorphous floods of primordial magick, and only the few and apart are capable of breaking free from the dimension's sway with their sanity still intact. The strongest of psyches have been shattered like fragile icicles, and the brightest of minds dulled into a simmer by its raw, untamable magicks.

Milo plummets deeper into the endless void of darkness and coldness.

The petite Hound numbs the fear enveloping the core of his soul. He falls deeper and deeper and deeper into the nothingness of the Microversity. There is no visible sign of a bottom, nor light, just infinite emptiness as he continues to dive aimlessly onto the abyss.

Soon, the Microversity's magicks drown his thoughts in emptiness and hopelessness. Milo loses grasp of his existence whilst the entropic claws of time hijack his consciousness. He becomes an abstraction, a meaningless speck deprived of solidity and sapience within the fluidity of the Microversity.

Milo, shapeless voices begin to call out to him. "Impossible"—Milo gasps.

Milo, the shapeless voices echo with a strange intimacy.

Milo, the shapeless voices pinch desperately at the frightened Hound's eardrums.

Milo, the voices call out tirelessly to the shapeless, fluid Hound.

Milo, pull yourself together, they urge him to retake his bodily self.

Milo, the voices awaken the Hound! They remind him that he is not the dream, but the dreamer. He remembers who he is. He is Milo.

"Come on, old boy, remember your teachings. Calm yourself. Calm yourself." Milo's thoughts resound mockingly across the vast, empty blackness. The Hound focuses and grapples for control of the Microversity's wild magicks. "Remember the Microversity claws and toys with your mind. Check. It numbs your senses, hoodwinks you into nonexistence. Check. And your soul practically becomes liquid, sloshed about like a whirlpool. Double-check."

Milo retakes his consciousness and bodily self, and the fears wetting his soul parch.

Milo stops falling. His tiny paws spoor the Microversity, and he smoothly lands on solid ground. At this point, the petite Hound simply sighs contently. But the calm is fleeting. The Microversity surges with raw magicks, traitorous and deceptive as the mind itself.

Milo, Milo, Milo . . . the shapeless voices resume their tired call from the nothingness. Milo surveys his surroundings. Darkness, endless darkness surrounds him. But the voices continue calling out to him, *Milo, Milo, Milo . . .*

He kneels, meditates, and mutely mouths an ancient incantation. A pillar of light swathes him. He flails his forepaws in a complex dance pattern. After images follow his fluid dance, creating the illusion of quick movement in a rippling blur.

The voices start to chant his name again, *Milo, Milo, Milo . . . show them old boy*, the voices become coherent and familiar, *Show them . . .*

Milo's forepaws never break their dance. Every move is performed with meticulous precision like a graceful dancer. A soft rumble quivers underneath his hind paws, and a cool breeze brushes his wet, black nose. But there is no actual scent, nor actual breeze. His imagination merely warps the Microversity's magicks into taking shape and form.

Show them what hell a Hound can wreck, little brother, the voices are of his brothers Iggy and Bobbie. Beyond the Microveristy's magickal influence they push him onward, enkindling his will further.

Milo proudly honors his bothers' appeal. He shows them what hell a Hound can wreck—what a Hound can truly achieve. It is as Grandmaster Harryhausen had said, the path laid before will be what you wish it to be. And Milo will do exactly that. Milo summons the magicks of his spirit, and he warps the fabric of the Microversity itself, molding its raw magicks to whatever he dreams up.

Shattered, kaleidoscopic images, as refracted off a prism, take shape and overtake the darkness with gleaming light. Material objects form around Milo, constructs of his disciplined mind. The Microversity's magicks bend and flex to his will like rubber, and endless hallways of shelves, books, and stairways materialize at the flicker of a thought.

A library of endless knowledge above the heavens lays before him—Milo's ideal vision of content and peace. A rhythm sets in, the Microversity no longer holds power over his psyche and name. Milo tames the unbridled fury of the realm.

But the Hound knows this is no victory, only a temporary mercy.

The Microversity is not tamed so easily. Whatever peace he has attained might collapse at a blink, and then he will be a slave to the Microversity's erratic magicks. The Hound slowly wavers, the strain to maintain the raw magicks at bay proves too great for his tiny physique. The wild magicks surge violently. They attempt to breach free from the petite Hound's snare.

Milo coolly meditates on his dilemma. He must conjure a way to escape the Microversity, his borrowed time depletes fast.

"Focus and be at peace." Milo distracts his mind from the crushing strain of subjugating the Microversity's raw magicks. Any vulnerability will prove fatal. Yet, freedom can only be achieved through a single, dangerous method. Milo wishes there were another way, but naivety won't do him much good at this point.

To break free from the dimensional depths and secure a way out of the Microversity, Milo must subjugate himself to the Aether Continuum.

A powerful spell wherein past, present, and future junction onto a singular conscious flow. A dangerous feat, but also the only means of breaking free. Regardless of magickal prowess or mental fortitude, strong and weak alike can perish during the spell's temporal tempest. A mind can be lost in the ecstasy of forgotten, youthful dreams or become catatonic from the shadows of things to come.

Milo takes in a deep breath. He meditates amid his library above the heavens. He summons the necessary spiritual energies and courage to survive the Aether Continuum.

He has never been a Hound to run and turn tail, nor allow his diminutive size to handicap his ventures or allow it to define his strength of character. He is determined to reaffirm his value and prove to the Horned One that he alone is worthy of inheriting his magickal legacy.

The petite Hound stands defiant against the fears plaguing his heart, against the shadows of doubt cast by all who have dared to question his ambitions.

"Okay, I'm ready." Milo proclaims aloud to an absent audience.

Milo joins his forepaws at the palm. A conjuring sphere appears beneath him. Its mystic sigils illuminate with golden magicks. His construct quakes as living darkness engulfs it. A powerful gust of wind follows thereafter.

The Microversity's ambient magicks vibrate with ferocity. A powerful force shatters Milo's library above the heavens. Wood, dust, and book debris fly abound. Ravenous, voracious growls echo hungrily. The library above the heavens is torn asunder. The Aether Continuum takes effect, and Milo finds himself before a golden, crystalline surface where powerful, enigmatic forces circle him from underneath.

The shadows dance around the petite Hound, who stands perplexed and bemused with the visions of ancient, mighty beasts. Then, far above the heavens, he witnesses seven celestial bodies come to be, emanating with warm, divine light.

Milo then hears loud, thunderous booms, and the golden, crystalline ground slowly begins to crack and shatter. The shadows cease their dance, and he bears witness to the first of three, living beasts emerge from underneath his hindlegs.

A gargantuan, feral monster rises, tall as the mountains, a juggernaut of a living force. It came to pass, and it goes out rampaging throughout the lands like a mad beast. Its yell is loud and bombastic, like a mighty and proud titan. The beast is granted the task to conquer and destroy across the globe with the force of an earthquake and, so it was, one of the seven celestial bodies perishes.

When the beast's cry fades to the void from whence it came, Milo hears another call, the second of three, living beasts emerges. It shines brightly, like a vengeful comet. It rises upwards towards the heavens. The beast spreads its wings. Its shadow casts across the lands like an eclipse. A false phoenix it is, for it brings upon a fiery red death. It is granted the task to scorch the lands, ablaze in divine fury, and so it was, as Milo witnesses the second celestial body fade onto the darkness.

As the second beast vanishes to the skies, Milo hears guttural hissing. The third beast rises from the shadows. A legion of fangs and serpentine, blue eyes swarm around the confounded Hound. Ravenous and voracious, the amorphous beast is given domain over death as it continues to lay waste to the third celestial body covetously. The beast is rapacious, demonstrating bloodcurdling bliss in its task.

Authority is given to the three to bring forth

an unfathomable holocaust through claw and fang and purging fires.

Milo, Milo, the shapeless voices, they begin to call out to him again. Milo is uncertain what to make of the events unfolding before him. He questions if the visions are anchored to his destiny or fragments of a time long past.

Fear and death are the only certainties as the Aether Continuum continues to carry Milo through visions of quietus beauty.

Milo, Milo, the shapeless voices beckon him, and a mysterious creature of flesh and fur suddenly oozes out from the Microversity's tarry shadows. The creature stands across from Milo, hunched over with a white, mystical aura rippling round its body. It is a gibbon who dishonors Milo with a turned back, and he chuckles sinisterly.

"It's you. What . . .? What are you doing here?" Milo futilely demands an answer from the gibbon, for he wears a familiar face.

It is Gideon the Lesser. The gibbon drools rabidly. There is a great deformity in the gibbon's nature, something from underneath. For Gideon's meat cocoons something, someone, ethereal and unknown.

The creature points to Milo. Its diamond

white eyes blaze with unmitigated arrogance, sealing their animosity. The nebulous creature speaks to the Hound through Gideon. Its oily, smooth voice seeps with an underlined craftsmanship for treachery and deception. "The storm has been unleashed by your paws alone . . ."

A powerful gust of wind surrounds Milo, and the possessed Gideon. Before he realizes it, both the Hound and the gibbon are overrun by a raging tornado. But this is no ordinary tornado. It surges with powerful magicks—rushing dust rakes Milo's tiny face and thickens to solid, hard stone. Milo soon becomes entombed within a derelict tower, corralled amid a swirling thunderstorm.

"Can you hear the cracks over the dimensional walls, little mongrel? Soon the walls shall crumble, and usher the extinction of this fictitious lie you inhabit." The possessed Gideon professes like a fanatic preacher to the confused Hound. The gibbon raises his arms to the celestial bodies and preaches to an absent congregation. "For the weak shall be devoured without mercy, the strong disenchanted and broken in their futile crusade. None can stop the divinely preordained convergence, the cataclysm foretold by liars and heretics."

The cold chill of death creeps down Milo's back to the tip of his white tail and to every tiny string of fur that coats his tiny body.

He tries to retaliate, but words do not escape his mouth. Fear of the unknown consumes the petite Hound. He merely feigns confidence and asks the one question that matters at this moment.

"Who . . .? Who are you? You are not Gideon. I am certain of this. You wear his face, but you're not him."

Gideon the Lesser is many things, a mad bigot, a mad extremist, and many other mad things, but never a mad zealot. The Hound senses a deep magick binding him to the being possessing Gideon. This strange newborn animosity continues to bloom between the two strangers.

The possessed Gideon stands upright like a Man and looks up to the heavens. Milo does the same. The fourth celestial body is purged of its luminosity, and it ceases to be. The storm dissipates, the tower begins to crumble down unto granules of sand, and the gibbon turns its cool diamond gaze back to the Hound.

"I am, but a dream, who dares to be the dreamer, rather than the dream itself," the voice buried in Gideon replies to the Hound's question. Its voice is wet with sorrow, and its form suddenly thins to dust that is carried off unto the winds.

Seismic booms thunder from the heavens above, and Milo witnesses two of the three remaining celestial bodies implode. Inert energies are unleashed, and in powerful, thunderous explosions, the fifth and sixth celestial bodies are next to be vanquished.

A series of events flash before him. The menagerie of chaos that ensues pushes the Hound near the brink of madness.

Seismic waves throttle Milo with dust clouds. Chunks of stone and gravel abound, striking him with blunt force. The Hound dodges the stones and tries to keep a fixed eye at where the celestial bodies once stood above the ethereal sky.

As the debris clears, Milo witnesses a conquistador's sword cleave through the gossamer walls of perdition, thusly jinxing an unsuspecting world with a spectral pestilence for a hundred years. A hand follows the sword, clutched to the hilt, ushering the conqueror himself—a man—who is clad in steel from helm to head and with ghostly, white eyes. Then, another man arises opposite of the conquistador. He is nude like a newborn babe, a man born colored with the fertility of the old earth and with golden, monstrous eyes that burn hatefully. Neither adversaries pay mind to the stupefied Milo, and they rush at one another to engage in an unfurling shadowy war of vengeance. A massive wingspan sprouts from the nude man's back and swallows both unyielding warring men in a ball of feathers which transmogrifies into a breathing womb. And even behind the womb Milo can still hear the thunder of their clash and he knows the duo of nemeses will never cease their feud till their bloodlines run dry into infertile deserts and the threat of extinction devours them both.

They continue to clash, until finally, the conquistador thrust his sword anew through the pulsating womb, unwittingly bestowing the miracle of birth, death, and resurrection. The putrefaction of creation is roused and the cleaved fissure on the womb erupts. Star children of immense power are birthed from death. The Hound can feel their rage burn bright as they rupture out from their prison.

Milo surveys the decayed fifth celestial body.

He stands before the hollow husk of a dead world, in the company of other glinting star children. In a blink of an eye, the star children vanish unto the vast uncertainty of time and space, ushering a new epoch of chaos. Two other worlds will erupt, eclipsed in hatred and death. But Milo can't mourn for the unknown, he only witnesses, and vainly tries to comprehend the meaning behind such wanton destruction.

I am death and chaos incarnate . . . and I see you little mongrel, a deep, raspy voice calls out to Milo from the slowly wilting sixth celestial body.

The Hound squints into the surging void and sees two cold, deathly eyes of immense size stare back at him. The creature from the abyss is ancient, a power unlike any that came before it. A scowling skull, the size of a planet, scorns the frightened Milo. The creature opens its maw and creates a powerful vortex. The vacuous force sucks in the asteroid remnants of the dead world into the pallid creature's gaping mouth.

Milo is unaffected by the powerful force. He remains idle, a helpless witness to an ungodly purge.

Loud, deafening shrills of despair consume the ambient air. The cries are ripe with fear and are silenced by death's dispassionate touch. The Hound's heart sinks with the weight of horrified realization. He never dared to imagine such horror.

The celestial bodies represented a manifold soul, worlds perhaps, sacrificed for some unknown, nefarious reason.

The dead shall remain dead, never to taste the miracle of rebirth. All shall return to the dark nothingness from whence it came . . . the cadaverous creature bellows with a rattling laugh.

Its maw creaks open again. A blinding crimson geyser spouts out. Millions of billions of translucent hollow forms gush out from the gaping mouth and stampede over and under Milo.

Milo knows what they are—the innocent souls sacrificed throughout the eradication of the celestial bodies. Suddenly, a sharp pain gnaws Milo's left paw—it crumbles like marble and shatters when he lets out a painful yelp. The souls continue to rush past him, and the Hound hears the squealing of swine. From the bowels of the cadaverous creature's maw, a herd of hogs gives chase to the souls, trampling and devouring them with sublime gusto. The hogs are unlike his friend Boreas; these beasts are savage, ugly, and monstrous.

The force of the spectral stampede lifts Milo off his hindlegs and sends him flying backward in a cartwheel. He spirals onto the abyss along with the millions of billions of dead souls and monstrous hogs.

Milo, the shapeless voices call out to him again.

Milo, Milo, the voices plead with him.

Milo, a bizarre, untold intimacy pervades in the voices.

Milo, the voices relentlessly continue to call out to him.

He comes to.

He has fallen flat on his face. Groggy, Milo stands. The landscape is marred with a haze. He blurrily surveys his new domain.

The Aether Continuum has transported him to a barren, mysterious dead realm. Milo cradles the space where his left paw once sprouted. He looks up to the skies and searches for the surviving celestial body but sees nothing, only a shroud of ruby clouds. The clouds begin to part; he expects to see the sun if not the celestial body itself. There is no sun behind the bloodened clouds. Like a watchful cyclopean eye, the moon, awash ruby pink, stands amidst the blood-red heavens.

Whether it is the true moon, or a foreign, interdimensional moon is uncertain. But Milo understands in totality the absence of the last celestial body. The barren, dead world where he stands is the last celestial body.

Milo, the voices call out.

The Hound discovers he is not alone. The voices have finally taken form. Three other persons accompany him in the forsaken realm. Utter strangers of an untold intimacy, their identities remain shrouded in shadow.

Milo, the chanting shadows, call out to him. A tall, powerful figure stands to his right. From what Milo can tell, it is a man. There is a heaviness of astute harmony within the man, a rootedness to antiquity, and everlasting courage.

Milo, the second person, stands before him. He is a young man of average size and subdued strength. A furious nobility surges throughout his being. There is much anger within this young man. He is self-loathing and broods with abstained ferocity.

Milo, the third stands at the forefront of the

rest. A red aura wreathes the person; she is a young maiden. Strangely, she inspires unwavering courage within Milo, for she is the living embodiment of hope. Mysterious power of an era long buried in abstraction dwells within the young maiden. She is a strong, courageous, and indomitable spirit.

Calamity and the scent of carnage permeates the dead air. The four strangers stand in unison, waiting for something or someone unknown.

Milo, the three voices chant.

An uneasiness he can't begin to comprehend gives sway to his soul. Milo sniffs a powerful presence all about him. It is archaic, a being who sprung to life before time itself—the barren world ripples at its mere presence. The unseen force brings forth otherworldly retribution upon those who foolishly stand defiant before its presence.

A bright flash spears the horizon. A silent explosion foreshadows imminent annihilation through divine, crimson light. The light descends upon the four strangers hastily, showering powerful magicks. It shines brightly, and Milo naively attempts to glance at it. The being is fury incarnate through heavenly, pure light; a godly creature with six wings spreads across the ruby washed heavens.

Its light grows more vibrant and hotter. The godly being speaks to the group of strangers. A high pitch ring needles their ears, the only sound lowly creatures such as themselves can perceive. The sound is deafening. Milo shields his ears with his padded paws. But the shrieking pitch can't be muffled. It bludgeons Milo's eardrums wet with blood.

Milo falls on all fours. Blood oozes from the ears, and tears soon run red too. The ringing grows louder and more unbearable. He howls in agony, a desperate plea for mercy.

The being of light dawns on them. Its mere presence scorches Milo's fur and flesh. The heavenly host sets them ablaze with a gentle flutter of its six wings.

Through annihilation, he is purged of mortal unworthiness. And he is finally able to hear the voice with clarity. The voice of a goddess, soft and warm, speaks to them.

> *I am the one true Mothergod. By my divine decree, I offer absolution. There is no salvation for a world callously immersed in sin, only abject*

retribution. Kneel and through the divinity of my light shall your sinful soul be purged.

The Hound howls in agony while every particle of his being are burned away. He returns to a state of ash as do all creatures upon death, ash that itself is disintegrated with the red flare of divine light.

Milo, the shapeless voices call out to him. He ponders on such a plausibility. The voices could not be. He could not be, for the goddess decreed them all sinful and were thusly purged by her divine light.

Milo, you can't give in. The young maiden pleads to the resigned Hound. *Get up, pull yourself together. You can't leave us. You can't leave me.*

"No, I can't go on. I can't. The pain is too great. So much pain, so much death will come to pass. I can't. I won't go through with it." Milo objects to the maiden's pleas, heartsick at everything he bore witness.

Life is precious to Milo, in all its forms and glory. To have witnessed so much death has taken a toll on the Hound's will. A blight has fallen upon his youthful optimism. Unable to see the light of hope, and feel the warmth of joy, he fears the shadows of things to come.

At this point, Milo reaches an epiphany. The events are anchored to his destiny; that is why he bore witness to it all. It terrifies him, knowing he will relieve the visions again in life, incapable of changing any of it. For one cannot deny the path weaved for them by the fates, a belief Milo fervidly holds.

"There must be another way. So many lives mercilessly slain. Innocent or sinful, it matters not, who are you to deny them salvation?" The Hound questions the goddess' decree, a question lost in the Microversity's cold darkness. He is defiant to stand idle as all life is extinguished without remorse or clemency.

But Milo quickly reminds himself of the visions. He and the other three shadows stood defiant, only to be snuffed out in a blinding, hot light. So, the divine decreed, and so it was.

"Who am I to refuse the will of a goddess? Perhaps we are all evil. Perhaps we are all christened in darkness." Milo ponders somberly.

Dramatic, as always. Light and darkness are two sides of the same coin, the maiden calmly reassures. Her confidence compels Milo to listen attentively. *One cannot exist without the other. Light is not by nature good, nor is darkness by virtue evil.*

"What are you saying? I don't understand." Milo, lost in somberness, broods over the inevitable death to come.

And this battle goes beyond simple platitudes. We must stand and fight. Everything we are is at risk. Our humble existence condemned to a lie, a fabricated dream. Her firm voice pleads the Hound to stand strong. *But we are not the dreamt, we are the weavers of dreams.*

"But we failed, laid asunder," Milo replies hopelessly.

Hope can never be purged or laid asunder. Hope is indomitable, the antithesis to the fear of eternal aloneness, the maiden replies in kind to the defeated Milo.

"Who told you such silly things? What fool preached such rubbish to you?" Milo queries with sublime sarcasm.

You did, the maiden's answer surprises Milo, sparking him back to life. *Now, open your eyes, my pup. You are the master of this realm. You just don't know it yet.*

Milo opens his eyes. Surprisingly, his body isn't charred, nor is he ash. He is whole and corporeal, floating aimlessly in the abyss of the

Microversity. He regains his composure and gasps in shock to the serendipitous turn of events.

"Do I know you? Have we met before?" He calls out desperately to the voice.

We have met, not in the yesterday, nor the today, but in the tomorrow, the maiden replies faintly. Her voice slowly fades onto the shadows. *Now go, break free Milo, keep on hoping, keep on dreaming, until we meet again in the tomorrow.*

Flabbergasted, Milo wonders if he still rides the Aether Continuum and if the maiden's voice is merely one of the spell's ruses. There is only one way to dispel his insecurities. He takes in a deep breath and allows his senses to take control.

He touches the solid ground again. Milo regains control of the Microversity's magicks.

Across the indivisible horizon, white light ruffles. Milo stands aback, skeptical, and afraid to relive the visions. Echoes ripple the vacuum of the Microversity. A lock unbuckles, a doorknob turns, and a door unhinges. A path materializes which leads Milo towards the door over the horizon.

Teary, Milo sprints on all fours towards the door, white tail wagging joyfully.

He reaches the door. Upon the first touch, he smiles. The door is solid, not a cruel hallucination. He swings it open. A fresh breeze brushes his face. The sweet smell of flowers and grass resuscitate his weakened spirit.

Milo does not think it over twice. He lunges out through the door, successfully overcoming the Microversity. The petite Hound never looks back, not even to see the door dissipate behind him in a soft mystic aura.

Chapter 6:
THE WISP . . .

Milo knows not for how long he has been unconscious. Minutes, hours or, dreadfully, days may have passed. He is uncertain at this point.

His eyes open to a blinding white light, and he tussles on reflex. Flailing his paws, the petite Hound franticly claws the empty air. Fortunately, his little wet nose calms his quavering nerves immediately.

The cool breezy smells of the forest are real and true, not magickal forgeries. He jolts up on all fours and heaves with a thumping heart. Milo still reels from his experiences within the Microversity. Nonetheless, he is relieved to feel the "real" again, and find his left forepaw intact along with his sanity . . . or so he hopes

Milo laughs aloud like a mad beast, proud of himself for breaching the nigh indomitable

Microversity. He rolls around the fresh, dewy grass, caught up in the ecstasy few can share with him, and bathes in awe of the natural beauty about him. No longer subjected to visions of carnage, annihilation, mad deities, and enigmatic voices, Milo has succeeded in the second trial and mastered the frailties of his soul and the unfettered madness of the Microversity itself.

"Okay, old boy, you're alive and somewhat mildly insane. Yet, 'tis no reason to act like a newborn pup. This is far from over." He pants, slightly uneased with the private conversation with himself. "Now, let's see where we are first, then on to what's next on the list of things that'll surely kill you."

He flings open the satchel and pulls out the flask and parchment given to all prospects before going through the doors and lunging onto the Microversity.

The parchment is nicely rolled and sealed with a wax engraved with Grandmaster Harryhausen's symbol, the Crescent Moon. Milo breaks the seal and unrolls the parchment to discover an annotation handwritten by the Horned One himself. He reads aloud the details of the third trial. The only audience being himself and the trees.

"*Congratulations, little Milo,*" the greeting sends Milo aback. The annotation is intimately penned and congratulates him personally on his recent success no less.

Milo ponders. Did Grandmaster Harryhausen foresee him making it this far onto the journey?—a question eerily answered when he continues skimming through the annotation.

> *No, no, please lay your misconceptions to rest. Prophesying and peering through the murky rivulets of time are not part of my collective gifts. I'd find life rather dull knowing all things to come, aside from the inherent madness that comes with such a dark gift that is. My, oh my, there I go again prattling on about inconsequential things. Now unto the task at hand. If you haven't noticed by now, you've been transported to Queen Mab's Forest. Your task is to appropriate faery dust from one of the faeries who inhabit the lush greenery. Faeries are fond of ponds if I recall. Careful, though, as faeries are known*

to enjoy their Pyre Dance. Get caught in it, and you'll be trapped in a catatonic state of eternal bliss and deceptive elation of which you'll never return— best of luck, old chum.

Yours truly,

Grandmaster Harryhausen, the Horned One

"What is it with this guy and mental torture?" Milo interprets a smidgen of sadistic humor lined in the Horned One's scrawl.

He starts to wonder if imminent death might have been thrown into the mix purposely, with no real intention to test magickal capability. Rather, for mere sick amusement. *Surely, Grandmaster Harryhausen, a most respected magus, is above this childish sadism*, Milo muses mutely.

"Or is he?" The Hound mouths incredulously. Without warning, the parchment dissipates in magickal green flames, lightly singing Milo's padded paws.

There is no time to waste in idle things, things well beyond his control. Milo has overcome the perils of the Microversity and is convinced none of the other two prospects have won the day yet. The Final Trials of Apprenticeship are still in full motion. He will rise above every challenge to be crowned Grandmaster Harryhausen's champion and apprentice, no matter what!

Milo composes himself and places the flask back inside the satchel. On all fours, he dashes deeper onto Queen Mab's Forest. The willful Hound has decided to weave his path, to keep on hoping, to keep on dreaming, and to see the tomorrows yet to come.

There is an old fable about the Queen of the Faery folk, it is not a fable shared amongst commoners, and contemporary polymaths sparsely broach the subject. Milo is a rarity. He is well versed in the fable, for he is partial to cryptic folklore.

Queen Mab, the mother of all, ruled over a menagerie of magicks. Flirtatious faeries, pantheons of immortal gods, are children of magick under the loving bosom of their mother, once upon a time. Her children, creatures of flamboyant imaginations, once ruled over sundry earthly kingdoms spun into existence from their yarns. Subjects of frail mortality and even frailer morality worshipped and paid them tribute with knee and blood.

Ironically, these creatures of Janus-faced magnanimity and everlasting beauty, were but mere subjects themselves, who paid tribute with knee and blood to their mother, their Queen.

Queen Mab's rule was known as the Golden Aeon of Gods. An age of innocence and purity. Both wise and benevolent, she ruled over the heavens, the earth, and underworlds for untold lifetimes. But as every aeon before, the Golden Aeon of Gods reached its climax when, from the great unknown, the first tribes of Men ravaged the lowly, sublunary realms.

Many believe the Queen of the Faery folk foresaw the darkness that tainted the souls of Men, darkness which in turn birthed all manner of monsters that ultimately cast a blight upon the majesty of creation. Others simply believe she was threatened and envious with the mere existence of Men who roamed free of her divine will.

Men did not create war, but it was baptized in the art through blood and fire.

A cataclysmic holy war was waged against the primitive tribes of Men. The once benevolent Queen Mab was overcome with bloodlust, bent on their extinction. But her children took pity on Men. Though fallible, they found them willful and capable of good. Soon Queen Mab's rule was overthrown as her children took arms against her, aiding the tribes of Men in their struggle for survival.

Disgraced and defeated, her very name and memory became embellished by myth and legend. As the First Aeon of Men dawned, Queen Mab faded onto obscurity.

Milo has studied the fable since he was a pup. He passionately believes there is some obscure truth to the myth. For many things, once thought to be mere fairytales, have turned out to be as real as the air he breathes and as true as he is a talking beast.

Before he dabbled in magick, Milo traveled the world, excavating ancient lands for relics and artifacts of antiquity. He helped unearth scriptures of ancient magicks and detailed scrolls of forgotten civilizations. Throughout dozens of expeditions, for as much as he hoped, he never found anything tangible to elevate Queen Mab from the shadow of myth and onto the light of truth.

Yet, the faeries still sing her tale, the tragedy

of Queen Mab. They even named the forest after her. They hold her myth as a tragic parable of the corrupt nature of Men.

Centuries ago, the world corroded unto an industrial engine, a hollow husk of its former natural splendor. On the Eve of Wakening, the faeries were the first of magickal creatures to manifest from beyond the veil of reality. Like vengeful Valkyries, the faeries spread across the globe, cleansing it of Man's poisonous engines and reverted the Earth's mutilated spirit to a reborn green purity. For the past eleven centuries, faeries have roamed blithely in the thick greenery of forest worldwide, protecting it from the poison of Men's blasphemous constructs.

Milo treks deeper into the forest, awestruck with its lush green beauty, and appreciative of faeries' magick. But he is precautious of the one rule Men and beasts adhere to: meet a faerie in the green, pay it nothing but the utmost respect.

Faeries are known for their aggressively territorial, albeit playful, and unwelcoming stance towards trespassers. They will charm any traveler foolish enough to overstep their bounds with their euphoric mysticism and ensnare them with their Pyre Dance.

The Pyre Dance is faery trickery at its most potent. If lulled with the spell, the sanctity of the soul will be violated, and its deepest desires exploited with perverse mirth. The unfortunate person, Man or beast, is then bubbled in an eternal dream of endless ecstasy, never to wake again.

None have ever escaped the Pyre Dance, nor have any been brought back from its hallucination. Not even Grandmaster Harryhausen has achieved such a feat. For faery magick is pure, untarnished by delusions of morality and desire.

As he makes his way deeper inside faery territory, the Hound is deep in thought. He replays his experiences inside the Microversity and mulls over the visions hurdled through the Aether Continuum. *What does it mean?*—he muses.

Everything was chaotic, and Milo is unable to decipher what was past and future and what lingers on the edge of the today. The sole certainty, regrettably, is the inevitability of the tomorrows to come.

Milo's heart swells with a cardiac of fear. To peek into the future is dangerous, and, as Grandmaster Harryhausen stated in his annotation, there is an inherent madness to it. Milo is shaken with the morbidity of it, to worry on what calendar day will the visions finally plummet him unto madness.

But time is of the essence, and he must not waste a single tick worrying about it today. He must focus on the task ahead. The pond is a few paw steps away.

The forest greens reflect with rich vitality off the crystal pond, and a fresh mist sprinkles coolly over Milo's little wet nose.

Milo's shoulders slump down. The unspoiled beauty relaxes him, but remains cautious, nevertheless. For all he knows, the faeries already work their magick on him, subduing him with a false sense of serenity. He tiptoes over to the edge of the pond. A ring of candles lays wilted and cold, long abandoned from a frequent visitor. Milo's keen nose snatches the faint scent of magicks.

Hounds' noses make them great sleuths when sniffing out different sorts of magicks and Milo's is one of the most gifted. He wiggles his wet nose a second time. Two different scents drizzle the air. The magick residue is of a simple pyre spell, the Familiar Requiem—a harmless spell used for summoning a departed soul. The second scent surprises Milo. It is of a familiar Man, Sir Nicolas Fitzroy. Milo thinks little about Sir Nicolas' visit to the faery pond. The old man is rumored to be an immortal who has outlived countless loved ones, never to join them in death. A tinge of pity pinches Milo's heart. No one better can benefit from the spell than a timeless Man.

Milo brushes the candles aside. He genuflects at the pond's rim and splashes a pawful of crystalline water over his face.

The refreshing spritz revitalizes Milo, seducing him into undressing and taking a small skinny dip in the pond. He lunges onto the water with a huge splash, unworried with being caught unawares by faery magicks. If only for a minute, he wishes to enjoy the peace.

A soft rustling over a thicket of shrubs tucked in between two Gog Trees yanks Milo's lazed attention. Nonchalantly, he swims out of the cool pond water. He shakes his tiny, furry body dry and dresses at a casual pace, cautious not to make any sudden movements lest his prying quarry gets frightened. He reaches for his satchel and pulls out the flask. He then carefully lays it down beside the pond's rim and, on all fours, Milo inches closer to the rustling thicket.

Creeper-like, he digs through the thicket with one paw and pulls the shrubs aside.

Silence. Then . . .

Beauty, unlike any he has ever or will ever witness again, graces his eyes with pup-like wonder. Dozens upon dozens of butterflies sprout out from shrubs, glimmering in the many colors of the rainbow.

Luminous creatures of indescribable beauty engulf the greenery of the pond. A Blue Morpho, slightly larger than the rest, lands at the tip of Milo's little black nose. The Hound wiggles it, giggling at the tickle the butterfly gives him. The Blue Morpho takes flight again, joining its brethren in the air. The butterflies gleam like silent pyrotechnics, circling Milo from above in harmony.

The Hound reverts to a puppy again. He smiles and laughs joyfully with arms spread wide, inviting one of the lovely creatures to land atop his open paws.

The Blue Morpho hovers next to Milo, and the Hound reaches to it with a single open paw. The Blue Morpho lands gently on the pad of his paw. It flutters its wings, drizzling blue sparks onto the air like pollen.

Milo smiles. He slightly tilts his gaze, enamored with its magickal beauty.

"This form disgraces your true beauty, milady. Please let us dispense of this lovely charade. Deception does not become you." Milo was aware of the faeries' presence upon stepping one paw into their territory. Hounds' noses easily prey on different sorts of magicks, after all, and, fortunately for Milo, faery magick can also be whiffed.

"Heh-heh" the Blue Morpho takes flight anew in a giggle. Its flight more fluid now that the Hound has called out her true nature. "Heh-heh, and flattery does not become you, little doggie. Heh-heh."

The faery sheds the guise of the Blue Morpho in a bright gleam to reveal a miniature being with blue skin, flowing long hair, and butterfly wings. She is a beautiful tiny maiden, so Milo thinks. The faery shudders with blue magicks, ordering her shoal of faeries to shed the masquerade. They obey and encircle the unwary Hound.

Dozens of mischievous faeries tease and corral Milo. Any other beast of inferior fiber would crumble in cowardice. But not Milo, though of tiny bite, he is more than able to back up his bark.

"Milady, please, you know why I'm here, and time is of the essence." Milo genuflects, to the faery, in hopes of indulging her pride.

"Watch yourself little doggie. A sugary tone will not mask the sourness of deceit." The faery replies whimsically to Milo's modesty. But the Hound knows better than to trust his ears alone. The faery's strobing glow flaunts her mistrust and ire. "So serious and dour, you're no fun little doggie. Heh-heh. You're in our playground, we alone make the rules, and you've no say here, heh-heh."

The other faeries continue to carousel Milo. They conjoin hands and delicately encage the Hound. Milo's no fool to the ploy at play or a bigger fool to outright challenge faery magick. The faeries' Pyre Dance has begun, and Milo decides to risk it all on a gambit of his own.

"I dare not presume to have a voice in your realm milady." The petite Hound shuns his romantic desires lest the faeries use them to lead him astray from horrific reality. "Please, let us not dwell in misunderstandings. I humbly beseech you for a dash of your faery dust."

"Heh-heh, so confident, overzealous little doggie. Pity, all we wish is to play and dance. Dance with us, little doggie." The wheeling, conjoined faeries form three expanding rings around Milo. The rings gleam like blazing rings of fire, with him at the center. "Heh-heh, hush-hush little doggie, forget the dust. Our boon can be far more... enticing. No misery or pain here. No foolish contest, no barbaric wars to misshape the flesh and soul. Only everlasting happiness. Heh-heh."

"Oh, milady, deception taints your fair beauty. Please, let us dispense of this lovely charade." Milo side glances the other faeries. They dance faster, and his shadow splinters into four dancing silhouettes. The faeries' dance intensifies, grows more luminous, and the Hound's buried desires begin to enamor his gaze.

And they play out before him.

Milo stands beside Grandmaster Harryhausen as his apprentice. No, as something more grandeur—as his equal. Peace reigns over the great continent. His brothers Iggy and Bobbie have each married and live out by the countryside with their flourishes whilst presiding over the Council of Suns as respected and revered members. Then there is Gideon the Lesser, who has since renounced his genocidal mission and devoted himself to the Shrine of the Old Green Ones—he is now an ambassador of peace for the Council of Suns. And Milo, ever the explorer, he penetrates the barriers of his realm to explore new worlds beyond the veil. The Age of Wonder continues for another millennium, and countless generations propagate unthreatened from the shadow of extinction thanks to the fruits of his efforts.

But it is all lie.

"No!" Milo rejects such childish fantasies. "The world's a dichotomous tapestry of chaos and harmony, beauty and horror, and life and death. One defines the other, and neither cannot exist without the other. And the tomorrow has yet to pass."

"Heh-heh, funny words, little doggie. Have you lost your noggin? Have the Microversity's visions finally made you go cuckoo?" The faery teases the Hound. She attempts to wane his resolve, but Milo resists the Pyre Dance—he fights off its enslaving euphoria.

"Come now, milady. I'm no fool. Deception taints your fair beauty and blunts your splendor." Milo grips to reality with every claw on his paws. The Pyre Dance may offer him everlasting elation, but it is a lie. He has since left childish dreams buried deep in the fathomless Microversity.

Fairies love to tease those caught in their dance, but Milo isn't like any other careless victim. His bookish hobbies have versed him well in faery habits and lore, and the Hound has earned the right to smirk with utmost arrogance.

He asks again, "why the charade?"

The faery glows hot. Her ire sparks violently to the defiant Hound's question. "Stop saying that!"

The faery is aptly ashamed of her angry outburst. Her magickal essence flickers, spouting a pinch of faery dust. "Heh-heh, you're incredibly good, little doggie. But a trickster cannot be tricked . . . it's too late for games. Heh-heh."

"I see. I shall speak my piece quickly, then." Milo stands, meets the faery's inquisitive glare, and plays out his gambit. "He used you, tricked you, and imprisoned you."

The faery's eyes flare. The Hound's boldness catches her unawares. She knows of what he speaks.

Milo cracks a small, timid smile. He has

her in his paws. "The betrayal alone wasn't sour enough. He made you his puppet and forced you to fulfill every selfish desire his barren heart coveted."

The faeries' dance intensifies, and Milo taps harder on the blue faery's painful history. Sorrow permeates her heart and bleeds out through her small, blue face.

"Stop . . . it's too late, little doggie." The faery's bubbly demeanor wanes. The dance grows hotter, and the faeries hum a lovely song of foreboding fate. But the Pyre Dance is nothing without the blue faery's magick. She has become enslaved to bygone sorrows.

Milo tenderly reaches out to the faery's fragile heart. "It matters not. I know why you do this, why you named the forest after Queen Mab. You felt a kinship with her, both betrayed by those you loved. Her children betrayed her and erased her very existence with their lies. Same as you. A loved one, a human, with no love to return except to riches and base desires, betrayed your heart. He forced you into servitude, humiliated you, so you punish all who enter your domain and drown them in their vanity."

The faery flies down closer to meet eyes with

the brave and stupid Hound who dares temper with her wrath. She feels something she has not felt towards another creature in ages—respect. "Heh-heh, you're a curious one indeed. How do you know me so intimately, little doggie?"

"Curiosity becomes us both, milady. I make it an effort to empathize with the dejected and downtrodden. What better way to do so than to reflect the pain of their tales through my own heart?" In the act of further humility, Milo bows to the faery with an arched back. "On behalf of all vain creatures, please accept my sincerest apologies, for you are but a victim, nay, a survivor of our less than noble natures . . . Lady Ariel."

With a simple wave of her hand, the other faeries cease the dance. Milo's gambit has paid off. He has appealed to Lady Ariel's sullen heart the only way he knows how, with honor and sincerity.

The Hound near collapses on all fours. The anguish to maintain a brave face and repel the powerful magicks of the Pyre Dance was vexing. But Milo is too timid to show vulnerability before Lady Ariel. The petite Hound is rather smitten with the blue faery. Now that the dance has ended, he acts like a clumsy, flustered pup before her.

"Heh-heh, clever little doggie." Lady Ariel giggles. She is amused with the Hound's sudden shyness.

"Cleverness had nothing to do with it, milady." Milo makes a mental note to thank Boreas should he survive the next trial. If it weren't for the parchments the Hog acquired ages ago from the Witch of Tumnus, detailing faery magick and lore, Milo would have never stumbled onto Lady Ariel's tragic tale. Though he wasn't entirely sure this was Lady Ariel from the outset. His blind gambit paid off indeed.

"On my honor as a proud Hound, I spoke purely, and my actions were just milady." Aware of faery's empathetic natures, Milo anticipated his actions ahead. He left the flask behind at the pond's rim to dilute any misconceptions of trickery and deception. "But I'm sure you already knew this."

"Heh-heh, you've gained my favor, little doggie. I shall now reward your nobility with what you desire the most." Lady Ariel said purely. The other faeries carry the flask over to her. She flutters her wings, and a sprinkle of dust sprays into it. "A little faery dust for the little doggie and a little closer you are to your heart's desire."

The faeries seal the flask and carry it to Milo. The sight of its glow etches a joyous smile across his furry face. He places it inside the satchel, gleaming with pride at his third accomplishment. "I can never repay you for this kindness milady, but if I may be so prudent and make one more request."

"Heh-heh, come now, you got what you wanted. No need for that silver tongue anymore." Lady Ariel is unaccustomed to such chivalry, from a talking beast no less. The Hound's sincerity and honor-bound demeanor are curious and charming to her.

"Yes, of course. Now, if I may ask, in what direction might I find the Marsh Dragon?" Milo is discomforted when Lady Ariel's luster suddenly dims.

"Oh, dearie me, the Marsh Dragon, you say. The Horned One truly is mad, to prey upon such a magnificent beast." Lady Ariel's voice is rife with concern for the dragon's safety, rather than his own. Not that Milo expected her to be concerned for a lowly creature like him instead.

"Um, pardon my ignorance, but why do you say that?" Milo asks.

"You don't know, do you?" The faery downcast a sadden look on the Hound, confusing him further. "The deathless man is to rip one fang off the were-jaguar, and that sinister fox is to pluck one feather from the magnificent nagual. Harmless little pranks, with no spillage of blood or souls maimed. But you, you got the Marsh Dragon."

"I, um, I—I'm afraid I don't understand. Grandmaster Harryhausen never explained what I'm supposed to pilfer from the dragon." He only asked to be surprised, Milo recalls. Perhaps he is to tame the untamable beast. No, the Horned One has a darker taste for showmanship. He will demand something far more grandeur, far more sinister.

Lady Ariel shakes her head disapprovingly. "The Horned One demands you present him with the dragon's heart. Little doggie, if you are to achieve your heart's desire, you must slay the Marsh Dragon."

The dark knife of revelation pierces through Milo's heart. He is expected to slay the great beast, an action that unnerves him even to consider. Never has he taken a life before, and he isn't quite prepared to start doing so. "I was not told, he—he failed to mention that part," Milo replies lowly.

"Oh, my," Ariel turns her gaze north and charms the trees and shrubs to part. A path through the forest is created. She turns back to Milo. Compassion gleams off her eyes. "Follow this path. It will lead you straight to the Ember Swamp Lands. Deep in the murkiest regions, through a mouth burrowed straight onto the earth, there you shall find your dragon."

"Thank you, milady." The Hound replies meekly. He is unprepared for what lies at the end of his journey and hesitant to commit the ultimate sacrifice.

On all fours, he starts to dash for the Ember Swamp Lands but stops in a jolt when Lady Ariel calls out to him.

"It is improper for a gentle-beast to leave without stating his name."—she says quite flirtatiously to him.

Milo looks to the faery bashfully. With a smile, he honors her request. "Milo Gabriel Mendoza, at your service, milady."

"May the Old Green Ones watch over you Milo, and may you not lose yourself in your quest." She replies sweetly.

He is left wordless, flattered a divine creature

like Lady Ariel shows him legitimate concern. "Thank you, milady."

In haste, the Hound turns and gallops onward on all fours onto the Ember Swamp Lands.

Chapter 7:

... AND THE WYRM

The Hound can't seem to brush off the uneasiness following him. The deeper he dwells into the swamps, the more his mind fiddles with the dragon's curious moniker. It resides in a swamp rather than a marsh. Yet, it is called the Marsh Dragon for some odd, unexplained reason.

"I suppose Swamp Dragon has a less charming ring to it." Milo thinks aloud.

No, it's not the dragon that has him uneasy, though the gnawing concern of dueling with a fire wyrm does make him feel rather queasy. In truthfulness, it is Lady Ariel's shocking revelation that has Milo feeling more than a rattling twinge down his spine.

To overcome his final trial and achieve his heart's desire, Milo is expected to slay the mighty beast. The Hound is prepared to do anything to accomplish his goals. He just never fathomed killing another creature for avarice alone and, much less, sacrifice his very soul. There is no honor in an act befitting of blackguards.

He faces a dilemma. Milo knows it to be pure idiocy to throw away this rare opportunity. No beast before has ever reached for such an unattainable honor with stride and talent as he has. An honor that might require him to soil his honor.

As he debates between his beliefs and desires, Milo wishes his brothers Iggy and Bobbie were there by his side at this very moment. They would know what to tell him.

"Stop being such a little bitch and do what a Hound does best." He smiles, voicing aloud what Iggy would most likely say to him.

Hounds are strong, prideful beast. Boastful about their natural sense of loyalty and courage. They are chivalrous creatures, protective of the weak and, even more so, their sense of honor. To achieve the greatest honor ever attained, Milo will need to betray his very nature. But he isn't alone in this venture. His brothers have been right there beside him through it all in spirit. To betray himself means betraying them as well, and betrayal isn't an option for him.

Smiling, Milo finally knows how to confront this moral dilemma. The only way a Hound should.

"With honor and true to thyself." Milo recites the Hound motto aloud with fervor. He bounds deeper into the swamps, uncertain of the journey's outcome.

The rancid stench of death permeates the swamp air. Decay and rot flare Milo's nostrils. He tries to scratch away the miasma, but his little black nose can't stop whiffing the palpable absence of life.

The Ember Swamp Lands are nothing more than a bog of putridity, an anemic land akin to a graveyard.

Milo shovels a pawful of the ashen, muddy earth, and inspects it carefully. The moist dirt is warm yet bare of any life. He can't find not wiggling worms nor roots suckling about for nutrients. The earth is barren and dead, unable, or unwilling to sustain fauna or flora. It is as if something robbed the swamp of its maternal soul. The Marsh Dragon, no doubt.

Pillars of hot steam jet out like a geyser from burrows speckled throughout the swamp, swaddling the coppice of Gog Trees with a thin layer of mist.

Milo's little black nose sniffs the ambient air, searching for the Marsh Dragon's scent. A vain effort, the stench of death is overbearing and cloaks the dragon's presence from his keen sense of smell. Regardless, the Hound is certain the great beast is nearby. Gog Trees are known to flourish only around the decayed domains of dragons. And the swamp is rife with them.

Curiously, a Gog Tree isn't quite a tree at all, but a large fungus bark. A few weeks back, Bobbie lectured Milo on the mythical healing properties of the Gog Tree root. The scruffy Hound theorizes that a single leaf cut of the root can heal any ailment, and cleanse the blood of any poison or toxin.

Milo knows his brother will be more than enthusiastic about experimenting with the Gog Tree root. But the root is a rarity. Not many dared to venture into dragon territory, not even Bobbie's courageous friend Zeke.

"Might as well since I'm here already." Milo tears three roots off from a collapsed Gog Tree. Its bark is obsidian black, whilst its inner flesh glows a warm orange, like frizzling embers.

As Milo places Bobbie's gift inside his

satchel, pillars of hot steam hiss out from under the muddy earth. He jolts backward on all fours. Fear tightly chokes him at the throat. For a second, the galvanized Hound thought the Marsh Dragon had gotten the jump on him.

If sweat could trickle down his brow, Milo would be more drenched than a soggy sponge. Though the swamp is moist and hot, the Hound's blood grows cold. He is a bit embarrassed for letting his fears confuse him. Grandmaster Harryhausen was right. He is but an insignificant mouse, a frightened one no less.

"No! I'm no mouse!" Milo yells aloud in defiance. "I may be a tiny, flea-ridden Chihuahua, but my bark can shatter diamonds like glass, and my bite pierces through steel as if it were flesh!"

In a surge of confidence, the determined Hound gallops onward on all fours. Piercing through the hot mist like a comet, Milo cements his pawprints in a long trail that spreads throughout the swamp's muddy soil.

From the Microversity's fluid magicks to the lush, seductive greenery of the faery realm, the petite Hound has matured much in a short span of time. There is still one more hurdle to overcome, and Milo is determined to win. He will conquer the realm of fire and death, the Ember Swamp Lands, and he shall emerge victorious in the Final Trials of Apprenticeship.

Milo stalls at the sight of burnt trees and shrubs. They appear to have been purged by fire. The Marsh Dragon's den lays somewhere nearby!

"Oh boy, it's now or never runt." Milo's fur coils at the nape of his neck. "Think Milo, think, what to do. Can't just barge in there all gung-ho unless you want to be turned into ash for real this time around."

Blind chance and vast bookish facts will do him no good this time around. Milo has never confronted a dragon, the epitome of power and fury.

The world around, dragons are held in high regard. Their indomitable, savage natures induce fear in the hearts of courageous warriors; and their thick hides are impervious to the most powerful magicks. Many vain attempts have been made to dominate and domesticate these magnificent creatures though nothing significant has ever been accomplished except a myriad of erected memorials to honor the uncivil souls who dared to rouse the earthly incarnation of infernal retribution.

No one has ever tamed a dragon, much less slain one. Rumors circulate though, that only the Witch of Tumnus has ever succeeded in charming a dragon. A rumor she neither confirms nor denies. Lady Tumnus simply reiterates the accepted truth, to tame a dragon is a fool's pursuit, for who would want to tame such power if not for vanity alone.

A dragon's hermit-like nature only adds further to their nebulous natures. Little is concretely known about these paradigms of monstrous power. And what little is known, is pure speculation. These handful of little-known things include: their scales are stronger than diamonds, a dragon's fire breath can liquify mountains like ice, and the only thing capable of harming a dragon is another dragon.

Milo has always dreamt about meeting one of these wondrous creatures from an academic standpoint, of course. The role of the dragon slayer does not mingle well with his sense of honor. But the stubborn Hound isn't prepared to resign from his quest just yet.

Finding the tallest Gog Tree, Milo climbs up to its topmost bough. He scans the field ahead with an eagle's eye. Just a few yards away, he spots the mouth of the dragon's lair. White steam gestates from within. The dragon is home for sure. A few more yards away from the mouth, past a cluster of Gog Trees, lays an open grass field.

Milo wags his tail excitedly. The gears in his mind begin to spin clockwork, a strategy is slowly being conjured. He wastes no time to rush back down from the tree onto the muddy ground below. He snaps a branch off the husk of a dead Gog Tree and holds it in his maw. Milo then rushes in all fours towards the open grass field.

The Old Green Ones, despite his lack of piety, have been kind to him thus far. He only prays they continue to smile down on him out of propriety. For this time, the petite Hound will dance with death under a blaze of fire.

Through a thinning pall of hot steam, Milo studies the walls of the dragon's den. Tunnel passages spread unto unseen depths. The den is a burrow dug onto the earth. Hardened stone has been shredded like sand. Milo deduces by powerful barbs, the notches on the rock are evincing to this fact. Furthermore, the den's erratic build is a testament to the dragon's ferocious temper. The fire wyrm is a force to be reckoned and respected.

Milo desperately sniffs the air. The hot steam makes it futile to pinpoint the dragon's scent, and Milo is forced to trek deeper inside hostile territory blind and vulnerable.

Light bleeds through punctured holes above the den, no doubt the same openings he saw earlier on the swamp's surface. Steam continues to hiccup from underneath the den floor. Modern polymaths hypothesize that long after dragon fire smothers, steam will continue to gestate unadulterated from the scorched earth for decades therewith.

The stone throat of the den sweats with droplets of water, dousing Milo's four paws the deeper he sinks into the dragon's lair. He imagines a dead river lying above the surface.

Milo's now deep inside the cave, and hissing pillars of steam become more sporadic. Brittle cracking sounds beneath his hind paws draw Milo's attention—he walks atop a cluster of charred, blackened bones.

All throughout the Marsh Dragon's lair, thousands of blackened skeletons lay atop one another in a mass graveyard. The skeletons are of Men and beasts alike. Lost travelers, scholars, and deluded fools dreaming of glory, the lot of them are the same in the dragon's eyes. Morsels fit for a monstrous appetite.

Hundreds of feet underneath the ill earth and still no sign of the dragon. Milo begins to doubt if the Marsh Dragon still nests at the Ember Swamp Lands. The echo of grinding stone and the soft, rumbling quake shaking his joints put to silence his yearning doubts.

Milo acts fast. The sounds grow increasingly louder, and the beast draws closer to him. He lunges behind a collapsed boulder; an age long relic from when the dragon first drilled onto the earth and crafted its den. The Hound takes a shy peek around the boulder to snatch a clear view of the colossal beast. A decision he soon regrets.

The Marsh Dragon is a fearful wonder to behold, a large serpentine beast more than a hundred stories long. Bony barbs protrude across its back from the head down to its tail, where a cluster of spikes creates a deathly bony mace. Its head is a beaked visage surrounded by a crown of spikes, and its scales feather outward like thorns all round its swerving body. A fiery glow in its marble-like eyes glints with the fire that flows hot throughout its throbbing veins. The Marsh Dragon's golden black-spotted hide is harder than diamond, impenetrable to any manmade weapon, and four pairs of hollow orifices run on the opposite ends from the base of its head down to its neck.

The Marsh Dragon's magnificent presence is hypnotic, spellbinding Milo with awe. But awe can prove fatal. Milo is careless. He forgot to conceal his scent from the dragon!

The dragon's orifices pulse excitedly. It sniffs the atmosphere of its domain and growls softly. Milo's stench has been caught! Its growl shakes the very foundation of the den. Granules of dirt and small stone pebbles rain down on Milo.

"Aw shoot." Milo looks around worriedly. He tries to devise an escape plan quickly. The Marsh Dragon slithers around the many crevices carved on the bedrock trailing after the Hound's scent.

Its fierce berserker growl drowns all sound across the cave. Milo acts fast. His mind always did grind ideas faster under pressure. He spots a small ledge slightly above him and uses the notches engraved on the bedrock as steps to climb up towards it. The ledge proves a safe vantage point. Milo now waits for his next move.

The dragon approaches the boulder and shatters it to small pebbles with a heavy swing from its spiked tail. From high above the ledge, Milo observes something of peculiar interest. An unwelcome surprise—shock even—glosses over the dragon's eyes when it realizes the Hound isn't splattered over the bedrock.

"Will the mouse succeed? You asked." Milo recites Grandmaster Harryhausen's taunt. He prepares to do the most reckless and suicidal thing of his young life. "Well, it's time we found out. Wouldn't you agree, ole Horn Head?"

Milo whistles to the Marsh Dragon. He gets its undesirable attention. If there is a single weak point on any dragon, it is their vulnerable, sensitive eyes. The dragon whips its fierce gaze to the Hound. Milo then catapults his tiny form straight at it.

He taunts the great beast. "Peek-a-boo!"—and gashes its right eye with his claws.

Milo bounces backward in an acrobatic somersault. He lands firm on all fours and rolls away immediately. Milo barely manages to dodge the Marsh Dragon's spiked tail when it writhes around madly. Its nettled cries pierce sharply throughout the cave.

"Hey, you, um, you overgrown maggot!" Milo taunts the dragon's aggression further. He hurls small pebbles at it along with his insults. "Over here! Come at me, turd muncher!"

Milo's strategy goes into play. First, he must lure the Marsh Dragon out into the open grass field. By flirting with the dragon's bloodlust, the Hound attempts to ensnare it in a delicate game of cat and mouse. His plan succeeds, and the dragon lunges in full force after him, eyes flaring hot with rage.

"Guess an apology is out of the question at this point," Milo whispers shakily. He dashes on all fours through the endless tunnels and bounces off the stone walls at every corner, with the Marsh Dragon speedily in tow.

"Oh yeah, I'm definitely off my rocker. Only a mad beast would've done something so asinine as to insult a dragon." Milo runs as fast as he can back to the den's mouth. He brushes through debris and steam in a blur. The Marsh Dragon lags dangerously close behind. "What were you thinking, Milo? What were you thinking?"

The dragon's roars echo untiredly

throughout the tunnels. Its protruding bone barbs grind and shred the bedrock further. Its mad rampage collapses stone pillars, compromising the stability of the den, an implosion from the underground will surely follow suit.

Its realm threatens to entomb them, but the Marsh Dragon's pursuit of Milo continues unabated. The serpentine monster is unconcerned with such trivialities. Milo focuses on the horizon ahead, afraid to look back and see the dragon gnawing the tip of his tail.

Surface light pierces through the pouring debris. The den will implode soon, yet a hollow sense of calm befalls Milo. He is close to the surface, with the dragon slithering ever closer.

The petite Hound lunges out of the subterranean den and makes a quick, decisive right turn towards the cluster of Gog Trees, intent on leading the dragon to the open grass field. With a powerful explosive gust, fury gores itself out of the earth—the Marsh Dragon makes a spectacular emergence from the underground.

"Over here, you, sluggish, um, worm..." Milo isn't accustomed to speaking rudely, much less boorishly. That is Iggy's area of expertise.

The Marsh Dragon's boiling glare pierces the Hound. Its eyes radiate with the blaze that runs deep in its veins. Its orifices pulse again, but this time something occurs. Pillars of fire jet out from the orifices in ascending order and length from the base of the Marsh Dragon's neck upward to its head.

"Aw no, no, no—this is much sooner than what I anticipated." Milo does not stand petrified in horror. He knows what comes next, and hastily runs to the cluster of Gog Trees and open grass field.

The pillars of fire merge and form a cobra hood around the Marsh Dragon's neck. A blazing breath of fire ejects from its mouth straight at the fleeing Milo!

The Gog Trees perish in a flash of ash, cinder, and fire. The force of the blaze thrust Milo on a thrashing flight across the swamp. He collapses in a rolling thud, barely escaping the raging inferno. The hellish heat blankets over his bum far too comfortable, and the burning Gog Trees collapse around him. He instinctively gets back up on his four paws. He ignores the scrapes and blisters over his body and resumes the dash toward the open grass field.

The Marsh Dragon does not let up. It is unwilling to let the trespasser go unpunished. It slithers onward, piercing through the moist, muddy earth with its massive body, tumbling burning Gog Trees down, setting off embers and ash to engulf the air.

"Come on, Milo. You're almost there—you're almost there." Milo's vision hazes, and the heat turns more unbearable. But his will is just as indomitable as the dragon giving chase. The open grass field is a few more paw steps ahead, close to the marked spot.

The Marsh Dragon pounces on Milo, using its beak as a spearhead. It barely misses the Hound by a small fine hair. The sheer blunt force sends Milo flying again, across to the open grass field.

He falls flat on his tummy. The chaos he has unleashed upon himself rings deafly in his ears. The dust clears, the dragon's yell rings across the swamp, and Milo stands groggily, meeting the Marsh Dragon's blazing glare from across the field. Certain death is upon him, and Milo only smiles.

"Oh, thank the Old Green Ones. Pity I'm a nonbeliever." Milo has landed right on the spot he had marked earlier. He looks to the dragon with a cocky smirk and taunts its fury with a single, waving paw. "Well? What are you waiting for? Go on, spray me with your sizzling spittle. I dare you."

The dragon's eight orifices pulse, blood fire rises, the pillars of fire jet out, and the cobra hood forms anew. The Marsh Dragon falls for the bait and shoots a powerful breath of fire at the petite Hound!

Milo gets in a defensive stance. He flails his forepaws in a complex dance, executing every move with meticulous precision. The jet of fire rushes at him. Milo outstretches his forepaws and, without a blink, welcomes the full force head-on.

"Pray I live *not* to regret this."—he calmly muses.

The fire mercilessly swallows him whole. The Marsh Dragon continues to pour fire on Milo indiscriminately, reassuring that not even ash is left behind. Its fury is appeased, steam hisses out between its fangs, and the Marsh Dragon coils back to admire the pyre it has unleashed on its offender. The admiration is soon marred with confusion. An anomaly occurs before its emblazoned eyes. The fire swirls. It takes shape and form, transmogrifying into a dome of fire.

A bright red glow shines from the muddy ground. Mystical sigils are engraved where the

Hound once stood while it was being incinerated. The fire dances around furiously, and the dome shatters into pillars of fire that pierce the clouds above with an explosive boom. Jetting embers spark wildly across the field, and the Marsh Dragon is sent into a berserk, confused rage.

Corralled in the pillars of dragon fire, right at the center of a conjuring sphere stands Milo—the fire's new master!

Milo's plan has come unto fruition.

His strategy was quite simple. Before entering the Marsh Dragon's den, Milo made a quick stop at the open grass field. He then took the branch he snapped off the Gog Tree earlier and etched sigils onto the muddy soil. The sigils were for a pyromancy summoning spell. Luring the dragon out to the field and goading it into shooting out a breath of fire was the tricky part. And then there was the uncertainty of his plan working out to the letter—a deadly chance Milo was willing to take.

The Hound flails his forepaws ceremoniously. Milo is master of the dragon's fire, and he bends it to his will, bringing the spell unto fruition. The fires converge above him in a brilliant flash, taking corporeal form in synchrony with his physical motions. The petite Hound hunches over on all fours. The fire swirls madly as four fiery paws form, then a tail and, finally, a snarling wolf's head.

The Fenrir Wolf is birthed from the dragon fire—a massive fiery construct tethered to the Hound's spirit!

The fire wolf takes a defensive stance and howls unto the air. It prepares to pounce the Marsh Dragon. Milo growls to the baffled dragon. The fire wolf imitates his commands like a living shadow of fire.

The dragon accepts the Hound's futile challenge with a dominant cry. It spits out another jet of fire at the Fenrir Wolf. The attack is ineffective, and the fire wolf merely absorbs the very fire that birthed it.

"It won't work!" Milo taunts, confident of his victory. "The fire belongs to me now, and so do you!"

Milo lunges to the air and takes a swing at the dragon. The fire wolf mimics its master's movements and knocks the Marsh Dragon down onto the muddy ground. A powerful gale sweeps the Gog Trees, and the dragon's hammering weight thunders over the swamps. The Marsh Dragon coils back up and strikes at Milo, but the Fenrir Wolf waylays its attack and pins it down with its fiery paws. The Marsh Dragon squirms to break free.

Milo's victory is affirmed; he needs only deliver the lethal strike. He hesitates, for a flutter of breath, and strikes with a gaping maw. The Fenrir Wolf apes the Hound's determination and bites down on the dragon's neck.

The Marsh Dragon writhes helplessly. Its breath smothered; the dragon fixates solely on the humiliation of being snuffed out by a tiny, insignificant mouse. The sheer irony, its fire, served as the key to its demise.

Milo briefly locks eyes with the dragon. The blaze behind its cornea dims like a withering candle. Sincere fear veils over the Marsh Dragon's eyes, and . . . with a wave of Milo's paw, the Fenrir Wolf melts away to lifeless embers. The Marsh Dragon rises quickly and hisses balefully at the Hound. But Milo stands unfazed, confident the dragon no longer poses a viable threat.

"Oh, I bore of these pitiful theatrics." Milo sternly stares down the wheezing dragon. "It's high time we chatted like gentle-beasts; wouldn't you agree?"

The Marsh Dragon lets off a guttural laugh and . . . it speaks to the Hound.

"Clever little mongrel." The Marsh Dragon says in a deep, raspy voice. It slithers closer to Milo and studies the Hound carefully. It chuckles, amused. "You're quite the curiosity, little mongrel. But you knew, didn't you?"

"That you were more than a mindless beast? Yes, I knew, from the moment you didn't find me behind the boulder back at the den. Your emotions betrayed you." Milo keeps a watchful eye on the dragon, careful not to let his guard down. The magicks exerted to summon the Fenrir Wolf, plus swimming through the Microversity and warding off the faery Pyre Dance has left him fatigued and spiritually drained. He prays the Marsh Dragon does not notice his exhaustion. "You know why I'm here."

"But of course, the Horned One has shared your intentions with me after all. You're here to slay the Marsh Dragon!" The dragon darts its glare down at the Hound. Its eyes flare hot with blood fire. "Yet here we are chitchatting like old hags instead. Well, what are you waiting for, little mongrel? You want my heart, go ahead, try and carve it out of me now."

The dragon coils back and slithers around the Hound again. Milo realizes the dragon's genuine interest in him, or else he would have been eaten by now. They study one another. The key to his survival now depends on keeping the Marsh Dragon's curiosity enticed.

"No. I refuse to take another's life for selfish reasons alone." Milo rebukes breathlessly.

"Selfish, you say? Great power was within your grasp, and yet you denied it simply because you refuse to spill blood!" The Marsh Dragon exclaims indignantly. It draws beak and fang closer to Milo's little wet nose. "You excuse your cowardice with delusions of morality, mask your lust for power with feigned altruism. You're nothing more than a cesspool of vice and ignorance, little mongrel!"

"I'd had you pinned. I'd won." Milo is vexed, worn from every death-defying feat. Death will be a merciful blessing, anything to end the dragon's goading. "Don't confuse my pity as an act of mercy. You're only alive because I allowed it."

The Marsh Dragon gnarls in laughter. The Hound's bravado would normally unhinge its fickle bloodlust, but today, the dragon is bemused. "Oh, little birdie, what a lovely melody you sing, a choir fit for the stupendously stupid. You forget, little mongrel. I am the monster birthed by the slumber of reason, so do not play coy with me. You will find that I'm not so easily fooled. Your soul is ripe with fear, and your words reek of folly."

Milo can no longer hold the façade of generous stamina. His joints surrender to fatigue, and Milo slumps face-first onto the muddy swamp grounds. He lifts his mud-coated head in a pant and smiles weakly. The Marsh Dragon has bested him in a game of wits. "Eh-heh, you truly are wise, mister dragon. Aye, it was a mercy I showed you, not pity."

"Foolish whelp!" The Marsh Dragon barks angrily. The Hound's confession spurns it greatly, and a spasmodic tail lash whips the ground. A dragon's hide is nigh unbreakable, but its pride is frailer than its eyes. "Did you honestly believe such bravado might earn you my favor?! That mercy might gain you a few more mediocre breaths of life?!"

His muscles ache sore. Yet, Milo nonetheless stands fearless before the Marsh Dragon. His eyes never stray from the dragon's blazing gaze. "To slay another for avarice alone, there's no honor in that. And a beast without honor is nothing more than a mindless animal."

"You know naught of what you speak, little

mongrel." The Marsh Dragon coils back and growls softly. It finds itself pensive over the Hound's curious nature. "Why throw away a rarity to touch upon a power beyond your mortal limits for honor alone? War is coming. Surely you know this. With the power you spurn, a mere whisper can eradicate this blight before it festers across the lands like a plague of locust."

Milo takes in a deep breath and drifts through the reels of joys and hardships he has endured in his short life. The people, both beasts and Men alike, who have come and gone in his life are remembered fondly. Lady Ariel's voice continually urges him not to lose himself. Despite everything, the trials overcome, the persons met and lost, the blessings savored, the horrors tolerated—the Hound has always remained the same, true to himself. He has grown wiser and limber, but his heart remains pure and beliefs unsullied.

"I saw the fear in your eyes. Palpable fear far evolved of primal instinct. You savored the omnipresent tang of death. To see that fear lacquer over your eyes showed me the price I'd pay to achieve my own desires." Milo cast a determinate gaze over the Marsh Dragon. His voice trembles wearily. "To sacrifice who I am and what I am is too high of a price to pay. I refuse to compromise myself—I refuse to cull my honor as a proud Hound."

The Marsh Dragon tilts its head in bewilderment and laughs maniacally. Amidst its guffaw, its forked tongue snares one of its fangs and pries it out. The bloodied fang is tossed at the tips of Milo's hind paws. The Hound looks to it with puzzlement and shock.

"You're quite the curiosity, little mongrel." The Marsh Dragon says purely. "State your name."

"Milo," Milo replies heavily.

"Milo . . . such a curious name for one so curious." The dragon's words echo Grandmaster Harryhausen's taunts from before. At this point, it feels like ages ago to Milo. "Take my fang and through faery fire, a mighty blade shall be forged for you. A blade not of war, but conquest. A blade to pare the veils of reality unto tatters. Impenetrable walls no longer confine you, little mongrel. That is my gift to you, Milo."

The Hound lifts the fang, a bittersweet joy. He threw away a dream but has attained a maker of dreams. "Thank you. I'm with nothing to say."—he replies to the Marsh Dragon's gift.

"You've amused me, little mongrel. Indeed, you have. Now, make yourself scarce, for I hunger, and from where I stand, you'll make a fine appetizer."

Milo gulps. Their tender moment suddenly sours. He takes the fang, ties it around his back, and dashes ahead of his muddy spoors, far away from the Marsh Dragon. His muscles are sore. No matter, the adrenaline will numb them.

When the Hound finally shrinks unto the swamps, over the horizon, and onto the forest, the Marsh Dragon muses aloud to itself. "Curious indeed. The Horned One spoke truly of you, little mongrel."

Chapter 8:

THE RUPTURING OF THE SOIL

The day turned out to be an overdrawn mess of mildly shattered dreams.

Milo arrives at Lady Ariel's pond seconds before tumbling half kayoed over the turf. The faery is kind and compassionate towards the world-weary Hound. She uses her faery magick to heal and rejuvenate his sapped meat.

Revitalized, Milo presents the dragon's gift, and when he confesses to having spared the dragon, Lady Ariel's teeny form smolders with jubilation. The faery surveys the dragon's bloodied fang with runaway wonder and caresses its surface with serene grace. It is harder than steel and surges with an innate power. Lady Ariel vows to use her faery fire to forge a magnificent blade of immeasurable beauty for him upon his return from the Horned One's citadel.

Lady Ariel then weights down grim news on him.

The Simian United Front has declared war. Gideon the Lesser unleashed an ambush against an envoy of peace led by the Stallion Commonwealth within the Southern Highland Woods. A brutal massacre of unbridled savagery unfurled thereafter. Gideon the Lesser used the unarmed envoy to make clear his intentions to take no prisoners during the ensuing war. Stallions and Men alike were torn from their limbs, and their bodies were then sewn together in a vulgar menagerie of chimeric carnage. Their blood was smeared across the trees as a declaration of conquest and war by the Simian United Front. The Chimera Bark Massacre, as it will come to be known down the annals of history, has sparked the fires of war.

The Witch of Tumnus has taken charge of the Council of Suns, calling for an immediate war council in the Republic of the Second Sun's capital—the Valley of the Second Sun. Gideon the Lesser spilled the first barrels of blood, from innocents no less, so the Witch is confident the gibbon has lost favor with crucial allies like the Heartwood Triumvirate and the Agrotera Empire. Pandemonium spreads across the great continent like wildfire, and much blood is yet to be spilled.

Milo refuses to listen any further. Words alone can't describe the terror which consumes him at hearing the eve of war sound its trumpet. The Hound isolates himself, cuddling in the discord of his thoughts. He drifts back to the outlying visions from the Microversity. The heralded holocaust has come whilst he slept, lost in dreams of hope, and Gideon the Lesser is destined to play a crucial part. A cricking chill runs down his spine, and effectively cripples him in a gloom. Tomorrow's dawn and genocide are imminent.

Milo keeps mum on the visions. He worries about the consequences that may arise should he share their delicate nature with another soul. The faery stares into the Hound's eyes with sincere concern.

Lady Ariel tenderly runs her mustard seed fingers over his cheek. Lovingly, she reassures the pensive Hound. "Worry not little doggie. Wars quell with time. Tragedies often shape the world and cleanse it with tears. A regrettable pattern that bedevils you, mortals."

Both rubberneck to the unreachable space

above. Stars nick the impenetrable dark thickness. The day comes to its natural end.

"Vow unto me little doggie, on your honor as a proud Hound, that you shall visit me here at my pond every spring from hereon. Vow unto me this itsy whim, my noble beast."— Lady Ariel demands cheerily.

Milo concedes to her wish gleefully. "I vow unto you milady, on my honor as a proud Hound, that I shall always return to you at spring's first moon at this very pond."

The faery smiles and joyfully whisks him away back to Grandmaster Harryhausen's citadel.

When Milo puffs out of thin air, Iggy and Bobbie yelp in unison then quickly become awash with joy and relief to see their little brother return to them unharmed and with his wits intact. Milo's jubilation is snuffed with silent queries if Gideon the Lesser's declaration of war has reached their ears. Given Iggy's calm demeanor, Milo safely assumes the contrary. He aches to apprise them on everything he has experienced, the war, the dreadful visions, but a magickally burnt spirit has left him too drained to broach the subject for the time being.

"Oi, you alright, runt? You seem rather down in the dumps." Iggy is the first to notice Milo's sour mood. As always, the gruff Hound's tender side sniffs out his little brother's grief.

"It's nothing. The day's left me more than a tad bruised and sore." Milo playfully brushes off his nanny of a brother. He then shows off his glorious gift and drops the Marsh Dragon's fang before them. A promise is made thereafter, and he will share its tale at sunrise's first peek.

Bobbie drools at the dragon's gift. "A dragon fang, you say. A rare gift like this is to be treasured, little brother. You've done fantastically, I say. The Horned One will surely elect you as his apprentice now."

"Of course, of course." Milo laughs half-heartedly. "I just, um . . . need to have one final private chat with him is all, you know, to go through details, ritual formalities and all that whatnot."

Iggy and Bobbie exchange concerned glances. They are certain their little brother withholds something or many somethings from them. Milo has never been able to keep secrets from either on his own. Fortunately, the gruff

Iggy and scruffy Bobbie silently agree to respect their brother's choices. They trust he will share his secrets with them at the correct time. After all, at day's end, Milo has gone from a timid pup unto a strong, proud Hound.

Milo's the lone Hound sanctioned entry to the citadel, so he bids his brothers farewell, though not for perpetuity.

Two footslogging Clay Golems escort Milo through the citadel's myriad of hallways and stairways. Strangely, the petite Hound misses the overbearing Artemisia. He realizes how much her barking livened up the citadel's stark atmosphere.

Grandmaster Harryhausen's private chambers lay at the citadel's highest tower. When they reach it, Milo sees Artemisia wheeling away a catatonic, Sir Nicolas. The blank, drooling expression on his face tells a dreary tale—the undying old man's psyche has become lost somewhere within the Microversity.

Undoubtedly, Grandmaster Harryhausen will be forced to enter the magickal abyss and recover Sir Nicolas' mislaid shadowy self.

The petite Hound considers the Horned

One in a different light. Perhaps he misjudged him, thinking him a sadistic madman. No madman is selfless enough to risk the dangers of the Microversity for another in distress. Alas, such reevaluated feelings are cut short when the Clay Golems halt by an ebony wooden door engraved with the insignia of the Horned One, the Crescent Moon. The doors swing open, and two other Clay Golems exit. The artificial giants drag a flaccid Religieux Marlfox, who spills strings of drool over the polished marble floors whenever he groans mindlessly.

Milo wonders what sort of hex befell the fox. Not out of concern, only simple curiosity.

Religieux Marlfox's jinxed stupor rattles Milo. He grows wet with fright about his private sit down with the Horned One. The Clay Golems reflexively grab Milo and forcibly shove him inside the chamber where Grandmaster Harryhausen waits for him by the study.

After seeing Religieux Marlfox, Milo convulses with the hysterics. He didn't slay the Marsh Dragon and dreads what sort of hex or jinx awaits him for disobeying Grandmaster Harryhausen's rules.

The doors shut behind, and Milo is now

alone with the horned magus, Grandmaster Harryhausen.

"Well, come forth, little dog. Come now, don't be shy, and take a seat next to me." Grandmaster Harryhausen invites the petite Hound in with an eerily calm voice.

Milo obliges, afraid of the consequences should he refuse the Horned One's hospitality. He sits by the magus' side, smiling keenly. Grandmaster Harryhausen merely lifts an inquisitive brow at him.

"So, little dog, I hear we did not slay the dragon?" Grandmaster Harryhausen asks nonchalantly. "Tell me, are these dangerous rumors true?"

Milo shamefully nods in return. Though he is not ashamed of the choices made, rather the utter contempt he expects from the Horned One, a man whom he greatly admires and respects.

"Now, why is that?" Grandmaster Harryhausen asks calmly. "Did you find my methods and demands so morally reprehensible, that you felt this yen to shun and disrespect my gift of infinite magickal knowledge? A prize many would argue is beneath the merits of a . . . dog, man's subservient pet."

Milo darts a scornful look at the Horned One, but flinches away from those blackened, nebula eyes and resorts to shake his head. He understands the magus only taunts him but does not quite understand the why.

"Come now, if not bark or bite, then at the very least speak up little dog. You've endured much today, little . . . Milo."—Grandmaster Harryhausen adds smiley. "Why not share it with me, then?"

The Hound's ears prick up attentively. For the first time, Grandmaster Harryhausen has called him by name. Milo finally looks up to the towering magus and finds not contempt, but curiosity greeting him.

"You've mastered the Microversity's chaotic magicks, charmed the whimsical faery, and conversed with a dragon and survived each experience, no less. Your bark has proven mightier than your bite." Harryhausen boasts proudly. "Still, no words? I see. Well, if you refuse to speak aloud, then let us whisper little Milo. Come now, let us whisper amongst ourselves as old friends often do."

Milo shies away from Grandmaster Harryhausen's flattering praises like a pup. It is all a tad too flustering, like a living dream.

"I—I couldn't do it, slay the dragon that is." Milo finally speaks up. The Final Trials of Apprenticeship are over, and he is no longer a prospect, but an equal of sorts. "To take a life solely for the sake of power and knowledge . . . my heart could not reconcile with that philosophy, milord. So, I politely denied myself the final victory."

Grandmaster Harryhausen takes to his seat and strokes his silver beard thoughtfully. He studies Milo with eager curiosity. "Sir Nicolas was leaps and bounds the most gifted, yet he failed to make it out of the Microversity. He became lost amongst the alluring reflections of yesteryears, and was unwilling to let go. Pity. It seems like infinite life does not guarantee infinite wisdom."

"Sir?" Milo is puzzled as to where Grandmaster Harryhausen is going with these intimate revelations.

"Religieux Marlfox, conversely, was a tad too assertive in his sinister quest. He siphoned the faeries of every drop of magick and mauled Lord Cuitláhuac. I'll hear no end about that lost eye for ages now." He pulls out a glowing blue orb from his desk. It is magickal essence bubbled in a glass globe, the fox's no doubt.

"You see, he had a sly notion to win or pilfer my magickal inheritance and exploit it for profit during the upcoming war. He wasn't as cunning as he boasted, for I was far more sinister. As punishment, I purged our beloved Religieux Marlfox of all magickal essence and memories."

Milo's heart sinks. He has briefly forgotten about the war sparked by Gideon the Lesser. Bloodshed was inevitable, as is his involvement. Grandmaster Harryhausen reads Milo's discomfort at the mention of the war but elects to leave the subject for another time.

The Horned One crushes the orb in his palm. He grimly explains his actions to the perplexed Hound. "His memories are no more, and he is left a waste of flesh. Now onto you, who has sparked much curiosity amongst us curiosities of the fantastic."

"I'm afraid I don't understand Grandmaster Harryhausen." Milo is unsure as to why the Horned One has kept him around after stepping down from the Final Trials of Apprenticeship. He refuses to lounge about as some novelty or a mere source of amusement.

"I shall illuminate you then—the victor shall be the defeated one." Grandmaster

Harryhausen smiles warmly at the stunned Hound. "The worthy one was to rise above each challenge not solely through sheer will or cunning. No, but through respect for the power I offer and the clout of fear to understand the inherent corruption that may arise from attaining such power. Only then would the worthy one, deny the close clutch of victory. And that is you, my defeated victor."

Milo is wordless from the welcomed shock. "I—I won . . .?"

"You truly have surprised me, little Milo." Grandmaster Harryhausen chuckles.

Milo wags his tail happily but stalls mid-wag. The Microversity's visions invade his mind. Milo attempts to share the sordid images with his newly appointed master.

"Grandmaster Harryhausen, as much as I hate to taint this wondrous moment, there are a great morbid thing I saw whilst swept through the Microversity's magicks—" Milo never finishes. Grandmaster Harryhausen lifts a bony finger and silences him prematurely.

"Hush now, it is not wise to concern yourself with tales yet to be told. For they are shadows without substance or breath, and the tomorrow is yet to be written." Grandmaster

Harryhausen's eerie charm calms the Hound, who smiles and resumes to wag his tail. "For today, let us go meet your brothers, we've much to discuss and a burgeoning war to oversee."

Both master and apprentice exit the chamber. The ebony doors shut behind them with a silent thud. The seeds of the tomorrow have begun to rupture the soil, and the Age of Wonder falls onto the dusk as the shadow of war looms abroad. But for today, at the very least, Milo basks in joy.

www.ingramcontent.com/pod-product-compliance
Lightning Source LLC
LaVergne TN
LVHW041637060526
838200LV00040B/1602